Top Dog

Top Dog

Emma Rea

Gomer

for Hamish

Published in 2014 by Pont Books, an imprint of
Gomer Press, Llandysul, Ceredigion, SA44 4JL

ISBN 978 1 84851 824 7

A CIP record for this title is available from the British Library.

This book is published with the financial support of the
Welsh Books Council.

Printed and bound in Wales at
Gomer Press, Llandysul, Ceredigion

Chapter 1

The last few seconds of the last minute of the very last day of Year 6 were ticking to an end. With every step Dylan took, the first summer holiday free from times tables came rushing towards him.

Dylan had had enough of school rules.

He'd had enough of standing in line.

He'd had more than enough of wearing a tie.

Six free weeks stretched out in front of him and he knew exactly how he was going to use every minute.

Matt and the others were yelling and jumping around, but Dylan fixed his gaze on the school gates. Four more steps to go.

Three more.

Two more.

One.

It wasn't until both feet were outside the school grounds that something in him exploded. Like Fanta spurting out of a shaken bottle, he raced off, unstoppable, away from school.

'Hey, Dylan! Wait!' Matt called out.

Usually they all wandered home together, nudging each other into the holly hedge, lingering at the corner shop, begging sweets off each other, but today Dylan flew past the hedge, past the shop and on towards the corner at the end of the road.

Just before rounding the corner, he glanced back. Matt was way behind. Tommo, Dylan's little brother, would be whacking his friends with his bookbag in the playground still. And the twins would have to go back into class to collect something they'd forgotten. Both of them. One after the other.

Just as Dylan turned back to face the way he was going, he smashed into something. Something both soft and hard. It leapt up and hit him in the face. Dylan lost his balance, fell backwards and sat, stunned and out of breath, eyeballing the pavement between his knees. When he could see straight again, he looked up. A boy a little taller than himself loomed over him.

'Uh... sorry, mate.' Dylan said, and grinned.

The boy said nothing. He had dark hair which stood up in glossy peaks and a face as blank as the paving slabs Dylan was sitting on. Dylan hauled himself up and bent over, hands on knees, to get his breath back and let the dizziness slip away.

'Never seen you round here before,' Dylan managed to say to the ground.

In Welsh villages like Dylan's everyone not only knew everyone else, they knew everything about them. What the best thing was about their bike, what their favourite dinner was, what they got for their birthday. Everything.

Dylan stood upright again. Excitement drained away and a cold feeling seeped through his gut as he looked into the most hostile pair of eyes he had ever seen. The boy wasn't grinning back. A sneer had begun to curl on his lips and he moved forwards, nudging Dylan out of the way with his shoulder as he marched off to cross the road.

Dylan shrugged and checked his palms for grazes. Not too bad. He wasn't bruised, just winded. He jogged the last few hundred metres till he reached the massive oak tree in the middle of the village common, then he turned and leant back against it to watch Matt racing to catch up with him.

Matt's freckled face had turned pink, his shirt hung untucked from his trousers and one end of his tie stuck out of his pocket. His breath came in great heaving wheezes, but his eyes were shining.

'Yeah – freedom!' Dylan said, and they high-fived each other, grinning. As a younger boy staggered towards them, they both yelled out.

'Three years later!' Dylan called.

'Slow or what?' Matt said. 'I mean, in your own time, Tommo.'

The smaller boy flopped down on his back on the grass and lay there, panting.

'I can't ever move again,' Tommo whimpered, rolling his big brown eyes up at the sky.

'Know what, Tommo?' said Matt, 'if a tortoise married a snail and they had you, they'd be disappointed.'

Dylan snorted. He settled himself down between two gnarly roots, with his back to the tree. The others came to sit either side of him, crunching old acorns as they sat. Soon, very soon, it would be time to tell them his plan.

Matt pulled a small crumpled paper bag out of his pocket and handed out toffees while they watched the twins, Aled and Rob, come lumbering into view. Beanpoles, Dylan's mum called them. They'd grown so fast they looked as if they'd been stretched and were exhausted by the experience. It took them forever but Dylan waited for them to fold themselves up beside Matt and catch their breath. At last, the moment had come.

'Know what we're gonna do this summer?' Dylan asked, sucking his toffee. 'We're gonna make a bike trail. A world-class bike track, a mile long, through the woods and round fields, with ramps and high jumps. We'll find planks and spare tyres and logs and stuff to build them.'

'Yeah!' yelled Tommo.

'Whaddya think, Matt?' But Dylan didn't need an answer. Matt was already nodding.

'You can see it, can't you? We're gonna start over there...' Dylan pointed to the gap between the old vicarage with the 'Ar Werth/For Sale' sign outside and the first cottage in the row that lined the pavement opposite.

'Behind the piano man's place...?'

'Yeah, then along the path at the back of the cottages...'

'Up past my house?' asked Matt.

'Yup.'

'Could turn off at Old Gwenni's house...'

'We'll do a loop round my dad's field first. We can build jumps there, if we go round the edges.'

'Then through the woods? Could bike straight through the stream...'

'Yeah, Matt, brilliant!'

Matt was the only one who ever got Dylan's ideas – ever since they were five years old. They had been digging tunnels in the sandpit at nursery school, not realising they were heading towards each other. Then their fingers had connected deep underground and they'd both looked up, astonished. After that, they worked together. When they finished digging and clearing one enormous tunnel, they jumped up, danced around like maniacs and had been best friends ever since.

'Cross the stream – yeah – hey – wait!' Dylan leapt to his feet and turned to face them all sitting at the base of the tree.

He was so excited, the last bit of toffee slithered down his throat before he had time to suck the sweetness out of it. An idea – the best idea he'd ever had – had just struck him. 'We'll go over the fallen tree trunk – that'd be so cool – cycling, balancing, along the tree trunk!' Dylan grinned at them all, expecting to see his own excitement reflected on their faces. But they just looked confused.

'Over the tree trunk?' Matt said. 'The one that fell across the stream by the rope swing?'

'Have to go pretty fast, of course – get some speed up. We'll saw off the branches and roots and build up ramps. With mud and straw and stuff.'

A silence hung in the air.

'We'll fall off,' said Aled, his long face looking even more worried than usual. 'We'll get all wet. Mum'll kill us.'

Dylan shook his head and sighed theatrically. 'If you're gonna get fussed about getting wet…' He looked at Matt. 'Should we let them come?' Matt stuck his bottom lip out and just shrugged. For some reason he looked as if he'd just been given extra homework.

'Be cool, Aled, or you can't come, right?'

'Can I make the track too, Dylan? Can I?' Tommo pleaded. Dylan looked at Tommo then at Matt. They both pretended to consider.

'I can't play on my own all summer, can I? And I'm nearly eight. It's nearly my birthday. I'm pretty strong now, look,' he said, lifting up his fist and twisting it to make his pale bicep bulge. Dylan laughed.

'Course you can, you big dufus. Come on, we're gonna need some tools.'

Chapter 2

With the others huddled close around him, Dylan thumbed the numbers up and down on the padlock till it clicked and the loop jumped open. The door squeaked as if it was in pain. It was dark inside Dad's workshop and all he could see were weird shapes hung on the walls or grouped in corners.

As Dylan's eyes got used to the gloom the strange shapes turned into tools. Saws with jagged teeth hung on hooks. Jerry cans of petrol were lined up beside a large metal bin, full to the brim with sawdust. Goggles hung sideways, silently watching the boys, and Dad's gloves, stiff and crusty with mud and oil, looked as if they'd grab you if you went too near.

'We'll need planks – get some of those back against the wall,' Dylan hissed at Aled and Rob. 'Matt – the mallet. Take those two spades, Tommo, and guys – we'll need loads of logs for tomorrow. Can you get some, Matt? Tommo 'n I can get some more from the woodshed tonight.'

Tommo was turning a handle attached to something on the workbench.

'What's this?'

'That's a vice, Tommo. Opposite of a virtue. If you've got a vice – which means a bad habit, like say, chewing gum in class – you put your hand in here, twist the handle and – see? – the edges come closer. Keep going and it soon squeezes the vice out of you.'

Dylan remembered his dad telling him this when he was about seven and he watched Tommo's eyes grow big, just as his must have done.

'Yeow! Argh!'

Aled and Rob were staggering backwards, clutching their foreheads. They'd been playing with a couple of rakes – trying to get them to do what they did in cartoons, so that when they stood on the teeth, the long handle shot up and whacked them in the face. Trouble was, it had worked. They both had a vertical red mark down their forehead and looked astonished.

While Matt and Tommo were howling with laughter, Dylan put his dad's goggles on and pulled at his shaggy yellow hair so it stood up wildly all over his head. He slid his hands into his dad's enormous gloves, swung round and yelled, 'Woaaarrrh!!!' right in Tommo's face.

Tommo shrieked, took a step backwards and knocked into the bin full of sawdust. He grabbed at it as he fell to the ground, tipping it over till it fell with a resounding crash onto the concrete floor.

He sat in a heap, shocked, with the bin emptying sawdust all over him and the lid clattering around and around. Gulping and blinking, still staring at the gloves on Dylan's hands, he swallowed, looked up at them all and managed a small artificial laugh. The attempt at laughing seemed to give him courage. He grabbed a handful of sawdust and flung it at Dylan.

'Squidface!'

Then another handful and another until they were all flinging sawdust at each other, shrieking and yelling and laughing as if they were in one of those paperweights which has a snowstorm if you shake it. It was surprising stuff. It stuck to eyelashes and lips, settled in hair and clung to clothes.

Aled flung it at Rob, Rob chucked more at Aled, Matt dumped a load on Dylan's head and Dylan managed to trickle some down the back of Matt's neck. Tommo just sat where he was, in the best position, flinging sawdust at everyone.

When there was no more to grab, they stopped. A thin layer of sawdust now lay all over the workbench, the floor and themselves.

'How did it get down my neck?' wailed Matt.

Dylan took the goggles off and shook his head and a few stray shavings of curled wood floated down to the ground.

'You look like a lion,' Matt said.

'I've got some in my mouth,' said Aled and Rob, with one voice.

'Those gloves are dead scary, Dylan,' said Tommo.

They stood in silence, looking around at the mess.

'Guess we'd better get this cleared up a bit. Matt – get the broom will you?'

Dylan tipped the bin down so Matt could sweep straight in.

'Aled, Rob, Tommo – scoop it off the workbench and chuck it in here, too.'

Somehow it didn't look quite the same as it had before, but Dylan couldn't work out how to make it any better. He hung the goggles up again, dumped the gloves on the workbench and ushered them all out with their planks and spades before clicking the padlock back in place.

'We'll meet outside your house tomorrow, Matt, straight after breakfast, yeah? See y'all then!'

'Bye, Dylan!'

'Bye!'

'And bring more logs!'

*

Dylan's mum had made his favourite tea. He put a huge forkful of baked potato, mixed with butter, covered with baked beans and topped with tuna mayonnaise into his mouth. It was a moment of such complete happiness that at first he didn't take in what his mother was saying.

'A new family's moved into the old vicarage, boys. I saw the removal lorry this morning. They've got a boy – he's going to be in the year above you at secondary school next year, Dylan.'

Dylan mashed his food until it was a pale orange

all over, except for the brown jacket of the potato, which he would eat after. Somehow it didn't seem right to say he'd already met him. It wasn't as if he could think of anything nice to say.

'You'd better go down tomorrow after breakfast and make friends. Ask him to go for a bike ride or something.'

'Can't tomorrow. We're starting the bike track. Maybe next week, Mum.'

'Well, the track can wait a bit, Dylan. It won't take long. They've come from the city, from Cardiff,' she said, pouring water into their glasses. 'There'll be lots you can show him – it'll be exciting for him to have all this freedom and space to play in.'

This time Dylan's groan was audible.

'Mu… u… um,' he said.

'What? I thought you'd be glad to have a new boy in the village.'

'A townie? Mum! He'll be scared of nettles. Scared of mud. Probably can't even ride a bike.'

If he was right and it was the boy he'd bumped into, he couldn't imagine him ever being interested in anything.

Tommo mimicked a townie holding handlebars and wobbling.

'Oooohhh… aaahhhhh… a puddle, oh no! My wheel's gonna get wet, oh no, mummy, mummy, ergghhh…'

Tommo faked a bicycle crash and disappeared

from the table, accidentally flipping his fork into the air so that it spun before landing, upright in the butter. Dylan started laughing. Tommo wasn't much good at anything, but he was funny. His mum wiped the butter off the fork.

'No he won't, don't be like that,' she said, as if it was normal for forks to be flipped up in the air, turn fourteen somersaults and then land dead centre in the butter.

Dylan began to shake with laughter, and Tommo just kept up his wobbling handlebar joke going 'wooo-oooo, mummy, mummy' and looking funny and stupid at the same time, in the way that only Tommo could.

But once Tommo was asleep in the opposite bunk, Dylan remembered the boy he'd bumped into. A cold feeling crept through his gut again.

Chapter 3

That Saturday morning, Dylan lay cocooned in his duvet, picturing himself cycling towards the fallen tree trunk across the stream. It was a question of speed – too slow, and you'd tip over, straight into the rushing water. If you went fast enough, though... He grinned, imagining the buzz once he reached the other side.

Dylan reckoned he could succeed at anything he wanted to do, as long as he had the tools and the time, and people didn't make him sit inside all day with bits of paper. Six weeks was hardly anything to build the sort of bike trail he wanted. But it was all he had before life closed down again.

He opened his eyes and stretched, and looked over from the top of his bunk to the top of Tommo's. They had a whole bunk-bed each, so they could both sleep on the top bunk and have friends on sleepovers. The lump under Tommo's duvet lay tantalisingly still, next to a blue Hotwheels car parked beside the pillow. It wasn't often Dylan got the chance to wake Tommo up. He picked up his own pillow and flung it as hard as he could. It hit Tommo's poster of the red Lamborghini, and dropped down with a sigh.

As if it had been waiting all night for the chance, the lump exploded. All Tommo had for ammunition were smelly, balled-up socks, stockpiled at the end of his bed, but he aimed well and got his revenge.

'Alright, alright,' said Dylan, 'just wondered if you were awake.'

'Huh,' grunted Tommo, sitting with his head in his hands on the bunk, feet dangling. Dylan dropped to the floor and pulled his hoody on.

'Get the wheelbarrow after breakfast, Tommo. It'll be by Mum's greenhouse, ok? I'll get Matt and everyone.'

'We're still starting today?'

'Course we are. Straight after breakfast.'

'What about the new boy?'

Dylan stopped putting his socks on.

'We'll do him first, then we can get on with the bike track,' he decided, shoving his feet into his trainers.

'Are you gonna let him come?'

Dylan stopped. He'd never come across a boy less likely to get his plans. But Tommo didn't know that yet.

'Don't be daft, Tommo,' he said. 'Just get the wheelbarrow, will you?'

*

Yr Hen Ficerdy – the old vicarage where the new family had moved in – was bigger than Dylan had thought. He and Tommo shoved their bikes up by the wall and went in through the metal garden gate.

They were about to knock on the front door when a strange bouncing sound made them stop, edge round the house and peer into the garden. The boy was leaping, arms stretched up high, on an enormous trampoline.

In mid-bounce, he noticed them. He bent his knees as he landed to stop himself and put his hands on his hips. His spiky black hair was gelled, to make it stand up, and his pale face stared at them with dark eyes. He wore white jeans and a thick, baggy hoody with logos all over it. Dylan was reminded of something, but he couldn't quite think what it was. The boy looked at Dylan and Tommo as if they had purposely come to ruin his day.

'Who are you? Mother!' he yelled, 'some of the village boys are here.'

He sat on the edge of the trampoline and swung his legs. The boy's voice sounded hard, as if he expected his mother to come out immediately. Which was exactly what she did. She wasn't anything like Dylan's mum. She had mousy hair and looked skinny and sort of hopeful and hopeless at the same time.

'Hello boys, what are your names? Come on Floyd, come down and say hello.'

She gestured at her son to get off the trampoline, but he didn't move. For once, Dylan couldn't think of anything to say, but Tommo managed to sound as if everything was going as planned.

'D'you wanna come on your bike with us?'

As Tommo spoke, Dylan noticed a huge shiny bike – with front wheel suspension – leaning up against a shed at the back of the garden and a smaller one behind it, which he must have grown out of.

'I'm Dylan, and this is my brother, Tommo,' he said. 'We live at the top of the hill, my dad's got the farm, Nant. My dad's a sheep farmer – he breeds prize-winning rams.'

He knew he was gabbling, but he couldn't stop.

'My dad's family has lived here for six generations. My grandad lives just behind our land, in Nant Bach. We thought you…' he stopped, then forced himself to carry on '– might want to come out. We were just gonna ride around a bit.'

His own bike was splattered with so much mud that you couldn't see what colour it was, and the seat had foam sticking out where Gramp's old sheepdog, Bella, had chewed it. Tommo's bike – which used to be Dylan's – was even worse. The new boy looked as if he couldn't think why anyone would want to do that. He shoved his hands into his pockets and looked away.

'But it's alright, we'll come back another day.'

Dylan grabbed Tommo's shoulder and turned to leave.

'No, don't go, please, come and have some juice,' said his mother. 'Come in. Floyd, you can show them your things.'

Floyd made a huge fake sigh, ran a hand through

his spiky hair and slid off the trampoline. He pulled on a pair of brand new trainers, zipped up his thick hoody and slouched past them with his hands sunk deep in his pockets. *That* was what he reminded Dylan of – a plastic model in the window of a clothes shop, all dressed up in the latest fashion.

'Follow me,' he called out over his shoulder in a low, drawly voice. Dylan grabbed Tommo's arm and pulled him back.

'Drink it quick, Tommo, ok? We're not hanging around,' he whispered.

They walked through two glass doors into a room so full of cardboard boxes you could only stand at the edges.

'We haven't unpacked yet,' said the mother. 'Why don't you open a few boxes and see if you can find something to play with?'

Tommo looked as if Christmas had come early. His eyes went all big and shiny.

'Wow, is all this games and stuff?' he breathed. 'And you, er, want some help opening it?'

'Yeah,' Floyd said after a long pause, during which he stared at Tommo. 'That's the robot box.'

'Matt's got one of those,' Tommo said, unpeeling the sticky brown tape across the box and pulling out a black and white robot, with a remote and hat. 'But Matt's batteries are dead,' he added, 'and the hat got lost.' He fiddled with the buttons and the robot whizzed and rotated and made a burping noise.

Dylan gazed out of the window. Matt and the others would be out by now. They'd be wondering where he and Tommo were. Tommo left the robot crashing into cardboard boxes while he and Floyd started opening another, bigger box.

'Remote control trucks,' said Floyd.

Turning his back on Dylan, Floyd pulled out a pair of enormous trucks with wheels as big as footballs and held them up to Tommo, who yelled when he saw them, scrabbled in the box for the controls asking,

'Do the batteries still work? Does it all still work?'

Dylan looked at the door Floyd's mum had gone through. It couldn't take long to pour three juices, could it?

'Two of everything. Wow. What does *your* dad do?' Dylan joked.

He glanced at Floyd, expecting him to turn round and grin, but Floyd kept his back to Dylan and the only answer he got was a dark red flush which crawled up Floyd's neck.

'Here, Tommo – look at this.' Floyd handed Tommo a transformer, showing him how it unfolded from a space rocket into a zombie figure. 'You can keep it if you like.'

Floyd seemed to have forgotten Dylan was there – not that Dylan cared. Floyd was opening box after box and at last found the box he was looking for.

'Rollerblades,' said Floyd, holding one up in either hand, gleaming, black and silver rollerblades, with tags at the heels for pulling them on and off, and a fat black rubber brake at the back of the one on the right, not marked, not muddy, not scraped. As good as new.

Dylan looked at them for just one second too long. Then he realised Floyd was watching him and turned away but it was too late. Floyd dangled the rollerblades from one outstretched hand. He ran his other hand through his shiny, spiky hair again.

'Haven't you got rollerblades? Like to watch me on them?' he asked, with a sneer in his voice.

Chapter 4

They had to go out through the garden gate, holding their pineapple juices in plastic cups, so that they could watch Floyd on his blades on the smooth pavement. Matt and the twins were already out, cycling around. The twins' foreheads had dark purple lines now where the rakes had smacked into them. A spade and a couple of logs lay on the grass.

'Hey, Dylan, we were just coming up to your place. Who…?'

Matt tilted his head towards Floyd. Dylan rolled his eyes.

'Mum said we had to come and say hello,'

He turned his back on Floyd and spoke so only Matt could hear. 'But we've finished. We can start the track now. Great you got some more logs.'

'This is Floyd,' said Tommo, 'he's got loads of stuff. You should see it.'

Floyd had finished lacing up his rollerblades and was struggling to his feet. He wobbled off down the pavement, arms waving, clumping about. Dylan longed to put them on, to see how difficult it was, get some speed up, see how fast he could go. But he wouldn't do as the others did, beg for a turn.

'C'n I 'ave a go? Give us a go?' Tommo was jumping up and down.

'Let's go, Matt, we can get started now,' said Dylan, pulling at his arm.

'In a sec, Dylan, let's just watch this.'

Matt shrugged him off and made his way down to where Floyd was standing by the post box, running his hand through his hair again.

'Cool blades,' Matt said.

Floyd inched his way back up the pavement, leaning forward and sticking his bottom out, with Matt walking alongside him.

'Does it take long to get that good?' Matt asked.

Dylan shot a glance at Matt's face. Good?! Floyd couldn't have been on them more than a couple of times before.

Matt's freckled face broke into a smile. Aled was hopping and jumping alongside Floyd, telling him how brilliant he was and Rob was just grinning. Then Matt went quiet and Dylan knew he was waiting for Floyd to offer him a go. Floyd slid down to the post-box again, faster this time, then stopped and stomped around to turn and face back up the pavement at them all.

There was a silence. Floyd looked at each of them in turn, as if he was trying to come to a decision. His eyes passed over Tommo's face and hesitated on Matt's, then moved on until they came to Dylan. He smiled again in that weird, creepy way and took a couple of steps towards Dylan. Dylan stared back at him, waiting, knowing what was coming.

The morning sun glinted off the silver stripe down the side of the blades, and the wheels rolled back and forth a little under Floyd's feet. Dylan thought they'd fit. He looked at the length of the pavement down to the post-box. A good run. He'd been ice-skating a couple of times, he didn't think he'd make a fool of himself. His whole body was pulling at him, tugging this way and that, squeezing him, urging him to smile at Floyd. But he couldn't do it. The smile wouldn't come. Quietly, so only Dylan could hear, Floyd drawled,

'You can't even stay upright in your shoes, can you?' Then Floyd swung round to Tommo with his creepy smile. 'Here, Tommo, they're adjustable. You have a go.'

'Yeah!' Tommo cried, and sat down to take his trainers off.

'No, Tommo – we're going.' Dylan said. 'Come on, Matt.'

There was a dangerous silence for a heartbeat, while nobody moved, then Floyd spoke in his low drawl again.

'Won't take long. After that we could unpack all my stuff, if you want to come and see.'

Dylan saw Tommo's eyes light up, and felt his stomach twist as Tommo yelled,

'Yeah, come on, it's great, he's got everything.'

'Yeah!' echoed Aled and Rob with great grins on their faces. Matt glanced at Dylan, then looked away again.

'Matt,' said Dylan. He'd never had to ask twice before. 'We're going to fix up the tree trunk, remember? So we can cycle across it?'

His voice came out sounding odd, as if he was begging or something. But Matt didn't budge. He just looked at his shoes for a while and scrunched his mouth up. Then he spoke.

'I wanna see this first.'

'Now, Matt, we're doing it now!' Dylan hadn't meant to shout, but everything was going wrong. Aled and Rob turned away. Tommo's face went red. Matt's freckled face went paler and settled into the brick wall expression he used when teachers were telling him off. A quick spurt of anger shot through Dylan.

'Forget about the track, Matt,' he said. 'And the rest of you. It's off for today. There's something else I need to do anyway. Thanks a bunch for the juice.'

He flung his empty cup at Floyd, expecting him to catch it, but it hit him in the chest and dropped, bouncing onto the pavement. They'd all think he'd thrown it at him on purpose, but he wasn't going to say sorry.

Dylan marched down the pavement through the group of boys and through the weird silence, fetched his bike and wheeled it back up again. He pushed off without another word and pedalled up the hill alone. Behind him, the boys' voices started up again, talking, asking questions. He even heard Matt laugh.

He stood up on the pedals, grinding them to go faster up the steep bit, by the village hall where Tommo would have his birthday party later in the summer.

They should have all been together, getting the spades and wheelbarrow, planning the track, deciding where the jumps should go – but that Floyd with his stupid playroom had gone and messed it all up.

Chapter 5

Dylan went to check out Gramp's shed for planks and tyres and stuff for the track. Gramp's dog, Bella, had had puppies a few days ago and Dylan still hadn't had a chance to see them. He'd heard the distant growl of Dad's tractor leaving the yard before breakfast and he knew his mum would be in the greenhouse, or watering her strawberries.

He cycled round to the back of the farm, to his grandpa's bungalow and courtyard. The curtains were still drawn but there was a gap and, peering through it, he could just make out the sofa with a scrumpled up rug on it. A couple of beer cans stood on the small table beside the sofa, along with a plate and fork. Another large table with a half-finished jigsaw puzzle took up most of the back wall. He didn't knock. Mum and Dad didn't like him going round too much, anyway. Gramp was a bad influence, they said.

At the other end of the cobbled yard, Dylan picked his way into the darkness of the wooden shed and found old Bella lying, panting, among a mess of chicken wire, planks of wood and faulty parts of farm machinery. Dad always said that Gramp's shed was a disgrace and Gramp ought to sort it out.

Beside Bella was the large box with one side partly cut away which Gramp had prepared for her puppies.

It was piled high with straw and Dylan peered at it in the gloom, thinking he must be wrong, she couldn't have had them yet.

Then he saw something. A dark splodge in the corner seemed to breathe, but it was way too big to be a puppy. Dylan tiptoed up close and crouched down beside the box. He was right – it wasn't a puppy – it was a whole heaving pile of puppies, melting dark forms all snuggled up together, breathing gently, their eyes still shut.

Every now and then a puppy wriggled or shifted, but didn't wake. They looked soft and warm and smelt milky. Dylan decided not to wake them. He filled Bella's water bowl from the outdoor tap, and sat stroking her head until she rested it on her forepaws and fell asleep. A piece of chicken wire lay by his feet. He picked it up, twisting it into new shapes.

Tommo was such an idiot. And Matt – how could he do that? But Floyd was the worst. There was something weird inside him – something cold and hard.

Being able to see straight inside people wasn't something Dylan had told anyone about. He had never thought anyone else would understand. But for as long as he could remember, he had been able to see what people were really like. Not what they wanted you to see, but what they really were. And not see, exactly, but feel it, deep in his bones.

Mum, for instance, was a strawberry, through and

through. She had pure strawberry juice running in her veins. Everyone should be able to see that. That's why she was so round and huggable and quite red in the face. Dad was made of engine oil – must have absorbed it through his fingers – that's why he was so good at fixing things. Matt was like marmite on toast – great if he liked you, awful if he didn't. The twins were floppy spaghetti with butter on and Tommo – Tommo was a custard flavour jelly bean. Not the flavour you'd choose, but you'd eat it if it was there.

Dylan's own blood was made up of all the fizz he ever drank, which was why it was so hard for him to think before he spoke, or to sit still and listen, instead of getting on with his own plans. But he'd never come across anyone like Floyd before. There was something ice cold about him, so cold it would take the skin off your fingers if you touched it. Hard, sharp. Icicles, needles, splinters of glass. As if his veins were frozen solid. The others couldn't see it, and Dylan wasn't going to start telling them what he was really like. They'd work it out for themselves before long.

The chicken wire he was twisting began to look like a figure, possibly a man. Dylan took his penknife out of his pocket and clipped some of the hexagons and twisted the ends. One of the puppies whimpered in its sleep. Bella raised her head and let it fall again. He found a twig of dead wood and snapped it so that the figure appeared to be holding a walking stick. It looked quite good. He made it walk along.

Across the yard, the door of the bungalow squeaked open on rusty hinges and Gramp's shock of white hair appeared, then the rest of him, leaning on his own stick. He grunted when he saw Dylan.

'Huh, Dylan,' he said.

Unpredictable, his parents called him and it was true. Dylan never could tell when Gramp would burst into a frenzy of enthusiasm, or suddenly become angry. But Dylan loved him anyway, loved the very skin of him, which was ridged and dark, like the bark of a tree. He seemed pretty calm today.

'Hi Gramp. When did Bella's puppies come?'

'Few days ago now. I was up all night with her, lad. She's not as young as she was. Seven healthy little pups she's got, bless her. She's a good mum. Six litters of prize pedigree sheepdogs she's had over the years, and I reckon that's about enough for any dog.' He bent down, leaning on his stick and fondled her ears.

'Too old, ain't we, Bella? This'll be the last time for both of us. We can go into retirement and watch clouds together from now on, eh?'

Gramp groaned and clutched his back as he stood back up again. 'Why are you on your own anyway, Dylan? What's up?'

Gramp was always blunt, too. Not one for brushing things under the carpet, Dylan's mum said.

'Nothing,' said Dylan. Then he shrugged. 'There's a new boy in the village.'

'And he isn't any good?'

Dylan smiled.

'He's a bit weird. He's got a lot of things – games and stuff. Everything I've ever heard of, in fact. But I didn't want any of it.'

He held the figure of the man out to his grandpa. 'Look. Do you like it?'

The old man reached out for it with gnarled fingers and turned it around in his hand. He chuckled. There was something comical about the figure. Dylan stroked Bella's head and she woke and licked his hand.

'Well, except the bike. It had front wheel suspension.' He picked up some more chicken-wire. 'It was all shiny – he's probably never been off road on it. If I had a bike with suspension...'

He stopped, picturing himself hurtling down steep banks and up rocky paths on a real off-road bike. 'It's dead unfair that he gets a bike like that – I'd really know how to use it.'

His grandpa began to make a strange noise, like a growl, and Dylan realised that he was about to work himself up. He looked up, startled, wondering if he had made him cross.

'Fair? Since when was anything in life fair?!' Gramp spluttered. Gramp's dark eyebrows had a way of shooting up under his mop of thick white hair, as if life was hilarious and full of surprises. He guffawed with laughter. 'Nothing makes me laugh as much as hearing people say they want things and not doing anything about it!'

Dylan stared at him. What was he supposed to do about it? But Gramp answered the question before it was spoken.

'How much would it cost, a bike like that? How much pocket money do you get? How much can you earn? You've got all summer. Do some jobs. Do something useful! Make something!'

He held up the chicken-wire man and shook him, so that the tiny stick dropped out of his wire hand. 'Fair!' he howled, shaking with laughter. He waved his own stick about. 'Don't just sit there moping, boy!'

He flung the figure back into Dylan's lap, and made his way, coughing a rich, gurgling cough, out of the courtyard back towards his front door.

Gramp's yelling had woken the puppies, who began snuffling and squeaking. Bella's head drooped as they wobbled towards her on rubbery legs, nosing their way to find a teat to suck, still full of sleep. Dylan picked up a puppy which was black, except for a perfect white ring around its neck, and rubbed its velvety fur along his cheek. It lay curled in his two hands, then woke and snuggled towards him, filling his head with a delicious sweet smell, nuzzling his face, hoping to find some milk.

'I've just had a brilliant idea,' he whispered. 'I'll come and see you tomorrow, little one.' He put the puppy down near the only remaining teat and watched it latch on, and suck hard.

Chapter 6

His mum's computer took ages to come to life. Dylan stared at the screen, willing the icons to pop up. He googled mountain bikes – and there they were. Better than Floyd's even.

The Muddy Springer had suspension and shock absorbers on front and back wheels. And hydraulic disk brakes. And twenty-one gears. Beefy tyres with such a large block tread pattern they would eat their way through thick mud, no problem. It even had a bottle boss, whatever that was.

Problem was, it cost three hundred and twenty pounds and he would have thirty if he didn't spend any pocket money by the end of the holidays. He scrabbled around the desk, found the calculator and tapped the numbers in. He was two hundred and ninety pounds short.

He took the figure made from chicken wire out of his pocket and turned it around in his hand. It was quite cool. It only took him ten minutes to make. It would mean an adjustment to the bike track plan, but Dylan's plans often needed changing along the way.

Maybe they could build the bike track in the mornings and he could find some way of working for money in the afternoons. They'd have to make the track much faster, of course. Then, by the time the track was finished, he'd have enough to buy a great bike to ride on it.

He slumped, letting his legs go straight and the calculator fall to the floor. It was impossible. Getting his mum to feed him Mars Bars and Fanta for breakfast would be easier than getting hold of all that money.

*

At tea that night, Tommo was full of news. Floyd had set up a sort of course in his garden. You had to bounce ten times on the trampoline, jump off and run round the pond three times, get on the bicycle (which had been left in the right place), circle the house, then do a cartwheel and kick a ball into a football goal. Floyd was timing everyone as they went round the course, and chalking up their scores.

'I won every single time! Once I even fell off the bike, but still I won!' Tommo's eyes shone as he recounted everyone's scores, which happened to coincide, as far as Dylan could see, with their position of power in the group, except for Tommo, who'd come first. So, Floyd always came second, Matt next, and Aled and Rob followed after that.

'Did you check his time-keeping?' asked Dylan.

'What?'

'Did you look at his watch as well? Or did he just call out the times?'

'Oh, he just called out the times. It's funny, you

can't guess at all how long someone's been. I didn't think I'd won, but I had!'

Tommo managed to frown at the same time as grinning. Dylan wanted to shake him. His own brother was being fooled. Floyd had made him win to buy his friendship. What a freak.

When Tommo was watching Dr Who after tea, Dylan went back into the kitchen, where his mum was making jam in a huge saucepan so heavy she had to lift it with both hands. The room was filled with steam and the candyfloss smell of boiled sugar and strawberries.

'What can I do to earn some money, Mum?'

'You could wash the car,' she said. 'I'll give you a fiver if you do it properly.'

She made it sound as if this was a wonderful opportunity. Dylan explained how much he wanted and why, and his mum stopped pouring jam into jars for a moment to turn and look at him. Her face was exactly the same red as the strawberry mixture in the pan.

'Two hundred and ninety pounds! You'll never get that much out of me, Dylan.'

'What if I wash other people's cars as well?'

'You can ask around the village, sure,' she said, scraping the last of the scarlet goo out of the huge saucepan, 'but that's still a huge number of cars. How many can you do in a day? In this heat? Four, maybe? That's if you can find that many people who want their cars washed, and can do four a day for three weeks!' She burst out laughing.

'Oh Dylan, I'd like to see you do that!' She screwed the lid down on the last jam jar as if that was the end of that.

Dylan left the kitchen and swung up onto his top bunk to think. Yes, an adjustment to his plan was unavoidable.

Chapter 7

Tommo was crushing Rice Krispies with his thumb. He was eating the ones he'd managed to pour into the bowl and exterminating the ones that had escaped, leaving little piles of powder all over the table. He drove a small blue car between the piles, slalom-style, then crashed it up against the Rice Krispie packet.

'We gonna start the track today, Dylan? Floyd wants to come. He's got front wheel suspension on his bike. Floyd says he can jump on and off benches with his. Or he's learning, anyway. Floyd says...'

'What? No!' As soon as the words were out of his mouth, Dylan wished he'd had time to think. Would it be so bad if Floyd joined in? He hadn't given it any thought. There was no going back now, though.

'I'm still busy. Maybe another day.' Dylan picked up his toast and chewed at it, not sure whether he was crosser with Tommo, Floyd or himself.

Back in Gramp's shed Dylan stumbled around among empty oil barrels, scraps of corrugated iron and piles of used agricultural bags until he reached the old bits of chicken wire at the back. He could still put the day to good use, even if they couldn't start the track. Some of the chicken wire had tufts of sheep's wool and muck stuck to it, so he had to fish around for a clean bit.

A stray scrap, already bent, looked more like an animal than a man. Dylan picked it up and squeezed some legs – what was it? A dog? A sheep, perhaps. He pulled off some of the sheep's wool from the roll in the corner and stuffed it inside his chicken wire figure. Of course it was a sheep. It would go with the farmer.

He sat down by the puppies' box, with a roll of wire nearby, cutting and twisting and shaping while the dark forms beside him snuffled and grunted and shifted in their sleep.

He began to enjoy himself. Tourists would buy them. They always wanted something to do with sheep when they came to Wales. If he sold them as a pair, a farmer with a sheep, maybe he could charge three pounds each.

Once he had twenty figures standing around him, each with its own sheep, he was ready. He needed some twigs of dead wood, which would snap cleanly to the right length. And a good few handfuls of sheep's wool to stuff the sheep with. The puppies were stirring and he reached down to pick up the one with the white ring around its neck again. The warmth from its belly heated the palm of his hand and he brought it up to his face to whisper in its ear.

'I know you can't hear or see yet, but when you can, I'm going to be there. I'll be the first person you see.' He held her at arm's length and studied her.

'Megs. I think your name is Megs. And you watch – I'm going to earn enough to buy my own bike.'

He put her back with her siblings and watched her snuggle back in among them.

He grabbed his bike, free-wheeled down the drive, swerved left into the wood and followed the path between the beech trees. It was cooler here in the shade and he could see better with the leaves filtering out some of the sun.

He wheeled over to the tree which had fallen across the river. It had a massive trunk – his arms wouldn't go around half of it. The tree was embedded into the riverbanks at either end but it had roots sticking up at the far end and branches reaching out where he stood. They'd need the big orange saw for the larger branches and once they were off, some tyres maybe, or planks, to build the ramp.

A little further on, by the rope swing, he noticed a sheep on the other side of the fence beyond the stream. It had pushed its head through the square wire fencing, and was nibbling the longer grasses which grew in the shade of the trees. The sheep saw him, panicked, and tried to pull its head back. It wouldn't go, and the animal froze, glaring at Dylan with golden eyes. Dylan cycled through the stream, which made the sheep wriggle and pull its head as hard it could as he approached.

'It's alright, silly old thing. I'll get you out of here.'

He eased one dark, woolly ear through the fencing, then the other, and that was it. The sheep came free and ran off.

It looked as if he'd come to the right place. There was a whole line of wool caught in the fencing as if sheep had rubbed themselves over and over. And twigs blown down in last Easter's storms were now dry and brittle and right for snapping into short lengths.

Dylan filled his pockets with rough twists of wool and lengths of twigs and was about to pick up his bike when a breeze made the rope swing sway towards him.

A small log, suspended from a high branch, dangled idly before his eyes. Dylan grabbed the rope, caught the log between his legs and swung out over the stream and back again. It was so quiet and cool and green under the trees and so good to swing back and forth, with his eyes shut, that for a while he forgot what he'd come for.

Perhaps he would let Floyd tag along. In a few days' time, maybe. You could see Floyd wasn't handy at anything – he and Matt would still have all the fun of making the track. Floyd could come and watch on his flash bike if he wanted. The others would soon see that Floyd wasn't much use, apart from providing a free toyshop.

Maybe they could use those old doors Dad said were taking up too much room in his workshop. He could just imagine Tommo's voice, yelling when a jump was done, 'Geeze a go, lemme have a turn!' He could almost hear him saying it.

Wait.

His eyes snapped open. He *could* hear him. That *was* Tommo's voice. He swung back and forth, listening. It wasn't in his imagination, it was somewhere nearby. And there was Matt's, too, and another voice.

He swung himself higher, to look out over Dad's field and saw them, right over there, at the edge of the field with their bikes and – what was that? The wheelbarrow? What were they doing over there? And why had they got the wheelbarrow?

Chapter 8

Dylan jumped off the swing, landed in a heap and slithered down the bank, then scrabbled up again to get his bike. He heaved it over the fence, and set off cycling round the edges of the field. He pedalled furiously, gritting his teeth at the thought of Floyd on his dad's fields. If they were building *his* track, without *him*... He rounded the corner of the field and skidded to a halt at the sight of the group of boys. Matt was holding the wheelbarrow and Floyd leant on a spade – one of Dad's spades.

'What are you doing on my dad's field?'

Tommo's mouth dropped open. Aled and Rob froze in their positions, like a photograph of people caught doing something wrong. The purple lines on their foreheads made by the rakes now had blue around the edges. But their faces weren't right – they didn't look as though they'd been caught out, they just looked surprised.

'What's the matter, Dylan?' Matt said, frowning. 'This was where you meant, wasn't it?'

'This was where I meant to build MY track. You can't start without me!'

'He's my dad too, Dylan,' said Tommo, not as if he was arguing, but as if he just didn't understand.

'Why don't you join us, Dylan? We thought we'd

build a bike trail around these fields,' suggested Floyd smoothly, and that was it.

Red sparks ignited an explosion in Dylan's chest and he threw down his bike and lunged at Floyd, grabbing his hoody and pushing him to the ground. He sat on Floyd's chest, pinning his arms down.

'Why don't you get lost?' he yelled. 'Why don't you just go back to Toys R Us you spiky-haired freak, and stay there? Get off my track.'

Floyd wriggled, but he was a useless fighter. His hair stayed in stiff peaks while he struggled, glued together with gel which stank with bubblegum sweetness.

'Get *off* me, mop-head. 'S not my fault you won't come along. Me and my mates are just having fun. Don't know why you have to jump in and ruin it.'

'*Your* mates?' Dylan got off Floyd and swung round to face Tommo and Matt and the others. Tommo's mouth was still open and it didn't look as if he was going to remember to close it. Aled and Rob were staring at their feet as if they'd only just sprouted them. Dylan could feel the blood draining from his face. But Matt's reaction was the biggest surprise.

'What's your problem, Dylan? Floyd is being friendly. Just 'coz you've gone off doing the track doesn't mean we can't do it.'

Matt's voice was harsh and his eyes were like a stranger's. As if he'd never seen Dylan before. Dylan was speechless. Could Matt really think that Floyd was trying to be friendly? Couldn't he tell that Floyd was saying the words, but laughing at him at the same time?

'*My* problem? I'm not the one with a problem, Matt,' he spat back, grabbing his bike and jumping on.

He shot down the path in the wood. Where was Dad today? Which field did he say he was doing last night? The trees rushed past as he cycled, small branches whipping at his face, his bike bouncing over the natural ups and downs of the path and splashing through the stream as Dylan crossed over. How could Matt ask him what his problem was? How could he not see what Floyd was like?

He came out of the wood too fast, onto the road and had to squeeze the brakes till they squealed so as not to crash into his father, coming up the road on his quadbike. 'Dad!' he yelled.

'What's up Dylan? Good grief, you nearly crashed into me. What on earth's the matter? Look at you, you're covered in mud and grass and stuff.'

'They're in the field by the stream,' Dylan panted, 'with the new boy, they're messing about, building a bike trail. Er – is that alright?' He never thought he'd ask Dad for permission for something at the same time as hoping Dad would say no. 'That's fine – as long as they keep to the edges and don't go near any machinery. How come you're not doing it with them? You're usually the one with that sort of idea.' Dad's face looked just like Tommo's had – like he just didn't understand.

'Yeah, right, Dad.' There was no point in trying to explain that the bike track *was* his idea. His dad waved an oil-stained hand at him – probably pleased he'd been generous with his fields – and Dylan watched him set off towards the farmyard.

Dylan wheeled his bike around and cycled back up the hill to Gramp's shed. The puppies were all sucking their milk while Bella lay stretched out beside their box. He slumped down in the baking sun with his back to the wall and yanked the sheep's wool and twigs out of his pocket. He tore at balls of wool and rammed them into the sheep. He snapped the sticks to the right length to make a walking stick for each of his twenty miniature farmers, each with his own sheep.

How could Matt just make friends with Floyd? Just like that? They'd started his bike trail without him! He picked up one last twig. And Floyd had actually invited him, Dylan, to join in! He snapped the twig clean in two and threw both bits down in disgust. Well, they could make their own stupid track. He'd make his own one once he'd earned enough to buy the Muddy Springer.

He looked over to Bella and her pups feeding in the hot sun and, knowing this new plan to build his own track was no longer big enough to fill all his time, he added another. He would also train Megs.

Chapter 9

'Mum, can I come into town with you today? You *are* going to the market, aren't you?' She'd been darting around the kitchen all through breakfast, gathering all her things together, getting ready to leave.

'Yes, of course, love,' she answered in the voice that meant she wasn't listening.

He took a clean dishcloth from the drawer and helped his mum load her jams and chutneys into the boot of the car. She was so busy counting them and checking the labels and telling Dylan she had a meeting at the delicatessen and that she'd meet him at about three in the car park, and then telling him it all over again that she forgot to ask him any questions.

At last they set off, and he sat with his rucksack on his lap, watching the fields go by, dotted with huge black silage bags, glad he didn't have to explain himself.

They drove past the grey stone clock tower in the centre of Machynlleth and up the high street into the heart of the market. It gave him the same old thrill – Wednesdays were always market days in Machynlleth, but Dylan could only go in the holidays. As soon as his mum parked in the Co-op car park, he yelled goodbye and was off.

Just about every inch of pavement on both sides

of the road was lined with stalls and the whole town was lively with cheery calls to passers-by from people selling things. Many of the stalls had red and white flappy roofs in case it rained – all of them were piled high with goods you could never be sure you didn't want to have a look at.

Dylan stopped for a moment at the toy stall with the huge red remote control Lamborghini Tommo always stared at. He wondered where he should set up his own small stall. He didn't want to compete with shiny plastic toys, so he walked on. Women would be more likely to buy his figures than men, so he kept going straight past the combat trouser stall. He was looking for people who had some time to spend, not ones who were buying useful things in a hurry. So you could forget the watch-battery and tool stall.

Cheeses. There was a queue at the stinky cheese stall, so people would be standing for a while, wanting something to look at. They could get a perfectly nice bit of cheddar in the Spar, just behind the stall, so they must be choosy, wanting something special, something really stinky.

He crouched down by the kerb where a good couple of metres of pavement were unused, and unzipped his rucksack. Reaching in, he pulled one of his figures out, and examined it. It looked so puny, so shoddily made. His chest went warm with embarrassment and he wondered whether he should give up right now. Someone from school might see him. Everyone he had ever known would probably come past and see these silly creations of his, and feel sorry for him.

He pulled out the dishcloth with a sense of doom, and placed his figures on it, in twos with their sheep, feeling stupider than he had ever felt before. He didn't bother unpacking the last few. It was a mistake, a stupid mistake. He'd sit here, staring at the pavement, avoiding people's eyes, for ten minutes, then pack up and go. What an idiot he'd been.

Shoes and boots marched straight past his tiny stall and stopped at the cheese queue. Once a pair of flip-flops paused, but only to stick a wrapper into the bin. None of them even slowed down as they passed him.

And then. A pair of pink trainers walked by. Stopped, and walked back again. Dylan didn't dare look up. Probably they could see the clock tower better from there. Probably weren't looking at his farmers at all.

'These are cute,' said the voice, and the pink trainers shuffled a little closer. She couldn't be talking about the cheeses. The trainers belonged to a pair of jeans, which in turn were owned by a blue canvas smock. A curly head smiled above.

'Can I pick them up?' she asked. 'Did you make them yourself?'

At least she was showing interest. She turned the figures over in her hand, and he felt grateful for every moment she continued to look at them. She handed them back and he felt a small thud of disappointment, until she seemed to be counting on her fingers.

'I'll take six,' she said, and turned to her companion, 'I'm always looking for presents for my godchildren.'

Dylan started to pick them out, but she crouched and began to choose for herself.

'I like this one,' she said, 'and this one because he looks so pompous.'

Dylan hadn't intended to give them different characters, but he saw what she meant, and realised that he could bend the others into more meaningful poses. By the time she left he had earned the first eighteen pounds of his life and the beginnings of a feeling of triumph.

He picked up each figure in turn to give it a character. He thought of the men he knew, his dad, Gramp, his games teacher, and moulded them all a little. He noticed that far more people stopped to look now that he appeared to be making the figures in front of them. Next week he would bring some wire and make more figures – that would free up more time as well as bring in more customers. A boy his own age with big brown eyes nagged his mum in a foreign language until she bought one.

Three teenage girls with their belly-buttons showing between their white tee-shirts and shorts stopped to giggle and croon how sweet they were and fiddled with them for ages. In the end they bought a pair each.

It went quiet around lunchtime and the man from the cheese stall came over to have a look. He was a stout man with a cheerful face and red cheeks.

'You can put one of your figures with a price card on my counter if you like,' he offered. 'People stand here for nearly twenty minutes sometimes, waiting to buy my cheeses. It'll be a sort of advertisement.'

He grinned and nodded at Dylan and went back to his stall and settled down with a cheese and pickle sandwich which Dylan could smell from where he sat.

A couple of kids with bright green ice-creams walked past and Dylan could almost taste the mint. Air gurgled in his stomach, reminding him it was his lunchtime, too. Mum would be far too busy to remember lunch. He wondered whether the stinky cheese man would offer him anything. Then he hoped he wouldn't – he wasn't going to let a single mouthful of that mouldy old stuff past his lips.

Feeling sorry for himself, he jangled the coins in his pocket, like Gramp did. Then he laughed out loud.

'What's the joke, lad?' asked the stinky cheese man between mouthfuls of sandwich.

'Nothing!' said Dylan. 'Will you watch my stall for a sec? Won't be a moment.'

He went into the Spar and when he came out, he was still laughing. It was like magic – one minute he had a few figures made out of scraps of chicken wire, the next minute they became golden coins and now, he held a Twix and a Fanta. The first lunch he'd ever bought with his own money. It was delicious.

He was draining the last drops from the can when something made him glance up the pavement. Beside him was a flower stall, where explosions of oranges, reds and yellows in various shapes stood in their pots in straight lines, and beyond that, the watch and tool battery stall. A tall boy, with hair slicked flat back against his head, stood in the queue, the next to be served.

Dylan's hand with the Fanta can in it stopped where it was, in mid-air, by his mouth. He could tell it was Floyd, even with the different hairstyle. For a moment, Dylan froze, trying to persuade himself that Floyd wasn't likely to come past his stall. A few minutes ago Dylan had loved his figures. Now that Floyd was about to pass them, maybe stop, pick them up and sneer at them, they looked puny again. They weren't programmable robots, after all.

Floyd was explaining something to the stall holder, who was nodding. In a matter of seconds Floyd would turn and come to Dylan's little patch on the pavement. The stall-holder held out a metal bar, about a metre long, with one curved end. Money exchanged hands between them and Floyd took hold of the bar. Dylan sprang into action.

He stuffed his can and wrapper into the bin beside him and grabbed all four corners of the dishcloth, dropping a few of his figures in his haste to gather them together. He grabbed at them, got them bundled up, slung them over his shoulder and was about to step onto the pavement, but he was too late.

Floyd stood, blocking his way, looking curiously at Dylan's bundle.

'You selling something? On the pavement?'

'No.'

'What's that then?' Floyd asked, smiling his sneery smile.

'Nothing. It's rubbish.'

'Rubbish?'

'Yeah, just a load of rubbish.' To prove it, Dylan crammed his bundle into the bin, pushing it way down so its contents couldn't be seen. He looked Floyd up and down, gave a glance of great contempt for his slicked back hair, and slung his rucksack over his shoulder.

'What's that thing?' he asked, nodding at the metal bar.

'A crowbar,' said Floyd. 'You *were* selling something, weren't you?'

Dylan shrugged and sloped off down the pavement through the drifting people. He'd managed not to look as if he cared but every step to the car park hit the question home harder—why, why, why? Why had he walked away? Again?

He reached his mum's car and leant against it in the sweltering sun, fuming, his arms folded. He wasn't afraid of Floyd. He shouldn't have budged. He should have stood his ground.

He groaned, going over what he could've done, things he could have said, how he could have handled it much better. He'd never do that again, he promised himself. That was the last time Floyd made him move out of the way. Next time, Floyd would be the one to move out of *his* way.

He was still chewing over his brief meeting with Floyd, waiting by their car in the car park, when his mum turned up, bright-eyed and dancing in front of him.

'Guess what?' she said. 'I sold everything – and the deli has put in an order for just about anything I can make! There's a call for old-fashioned, home-made jams and chutneys. They sell fast and the deli can't get enough of them!' Dylan grinned back at her.

'Great, Mum.'

'You alright? What've you been doing?'

It made Dylan remember his own success and, feeling a bit foolish, he held out his coins in one hand and the remaining figures from his rucksack in the other.

'No!' she cried, 'I don't believe it! That's brilliant Dylan!'

By the time Dylan was home he had thirty fat gold coins jangling in his pocket – as much in one day as his whole summer's pocket money.

He raced up to the puppy shed, bursting with his

news. Megs was shuffling around and he picked her up and saw that her eyelids had opened to show two dark blue sleepy eyes. It didn't look as if she could see very well yet and he knew it'd be a few days before she could hear him. But it seemed like a good time for a proper introduction.

'Hello Megs. It's me, Dylan. I'm going to be a millionaire.'

Chapter 10

'Mum? Can I have one more person to my birthday party?' Tommo asked.

Dylan stuck his fork into the tangled swirls of spaghetti and twisted it round and round. He was making a point of not watching Tommo, who held his fork, dripping with spaghetti, up high and tipped his head back so the longest strands could slither into his mouth first. Of all the methods of eating spaghetti, it was the least messy Tommo had ever tried.

'You've already got your whole class and the village. Who else do you want?'

'Floyd, of course.'

Dylan stopped chewing.

'You can't ask him,' said Dylan.

'What do you mean, he can't?' said his mum. 'Of course he can. We can't leave him out.'

'Why not? Just because he's come to the village doesn't mean we have to like him, does it?'

'I think it means we have to try, Dylan.'

'We don't! We really don't!'

'I do like him, anyway,' said Tommo, 'and it's my party.'

'If you invite that creep to your party, then I'm not coming.' Mum and Tommo were staring at him.

'Dylan? Of course you're coming.'

'Are you Dylan? You will, won't you?' Tommo looked worried.

'Not if he is.' He put his plate into the dishwasher and crashed the door shut so that all the crockery rattled inside. His mum's voice called after him as he banged the front door and jumped on his bike. He didn't know where he was going and he didn't care. He cycled down the hill towards the common, then stopped, not wanting to go too close to Floyd's house.

Dumping his bike, he sat on the low wall outside Old Gwenni's house, kicking, making trails of plaster from the wall crumble to the pavement. Her curtains twitched and he turned round so that he wouldn't have to wave to her, but she came out of her front door and soft footsteps shuffled up the little garden path.

'Hello Dylan, *'machgen i.'* She always called him that – *'machgen i,* my boy. 'Something wrong?'

'No.' He turned away.

'Come in and have a juice, my boy, and tell me about school.'

'I've left school. Going to the secondary in September.' It was all he could do to give her this much information. 'Might not even go then. I'm working now. Looking for work in fact. Was going to knock on your door and see if your car needs a wash.'

He turned to look at her wrinkled face and bright blue twinkly eyes and brilliant white hair, which stuck out in all directions like an afro. She had milky tea with three sugars running through her veins – you could see that straight off. It must be so easy being old. Just loads of T.V. to watch and cake to eat.

'Ooh, you're just the man for the job,' she said, catching hold of his wrist. 'Come with me, Dylan lad.'

She pulled him through her house into her back garden. Long grasses and dandelions and buttercups blew to and fro in the evening breeze. She seemed to be excited about something – she was bustling about at twice her normal speed. She opened the door to the shed and stood back so Dylan could go in.

'Look at that!' she said.

A lawn-mower stood there, brand new, red and shiny, gleaming in the light which came in through the shed door. 'My Bobby gave it me for my birthday and I can't use it. My wrists just haven't the strength in them. And look at the state of my lawn, will you?'

Together they worked out where the leads went and which order the buttons had to be pressed. He mowed her tiny garden once on a high setting and then again, on a lower one. It looked a fresher, brighter green when he'd finished. And he was so thirsty that he couldn't think about still feeling angry with Tommo.

She brought him some home-made lemonade which was nearly as good as Fanta, and a plate with chocolate biscuits on. Dylan handed his glass back and thanked her, and tried to walk back through her house without leaving a trail of grassy footprints. At the door she put a five pound note in his hand and asked him to come back each week through the summer, her eyes all twinkly again.

'Thank you dear,' she said, 'you've done a great job.'

Dylan rode back up the hill in the evening light. The heat of the day had turned into a gentle warmth and he could see swallows swooping in and out of the barn eaves. Before he got home, he saw a figure some distance away, walking through the woods, waving a stick from side to side. Sliding off his bike he wheeled it closer, stopping beside a holly bush.

It was Floyd, walking between the trees, head bent low. He wasn't waving a stick, he was swinging the crowbar from side to side. Suddenly he stopped, raised his arm high and whacked the crowbar into the massive trunk of a tree as if he thought he could fell it with one blow. He didn't seem to be in a temper, but there was a cold, deliberate anger about his movements.

Dylan shrank back. Floyd stood still for a while, then raised the crowbar again and brought it crashing down with another almighty blow. Even from this distance, Dylan felt the chill coming off Floyd. He backed off and cycled the rest of the way up the hill, pedalling at top speed.

Banging open the front door, he yelled 'I'm back!' and his mum came out of the kitchen drying her hands on a dishcloth.

'You've cheered up. You might go and see if you can do the same for Tommo – he's very upset.'

Dylan opened the bedroom door without letting the handle spring back and squeak. The lump on Tommo's top bunk didn't move. Dylan pictured Tommo's birthday party and how miserable he would feel if he missed it. Then he imagined what it would be like if he went and Floyd was there.

A vision of Floyd walloping the tree in cold fury flashed past his eyes. Why was he the only person who could see that something was wrong – badly wrong – with Floyd? He went to brush his teeth and stared into his own clear brown eyes in the mirror. He sometimes wondered if anyone could tell from his eyes that he could see inside people. He couldn't see anything different himself.

He tried to squash his sandy hair back into place, then gave up.

Back in the bedroom he stood beside Tommo's bunk. He was just about to whisper Tommo's name when he pictured Floyd sneering at him, hanging out with all *his* friends, and stopped.

He undressed in silence and climbed into his bunk without saying a word.

Chapter 11

It was simple to get work after that. He knocked on each door in the village and asked if he could mow their lawn, or wash the car. Mostly, it was old ladies who said he could mow and a few men said he could wash their cars.

For six solid days he was busy. The sun grew hotter and hotter and cars dazzled him as he washed them. Each lawn mower worked in its own way and the older ones needed a bit of a knack to get them going.

Just before tea each day he'd go up to the puppies and check on Megs. Gramp would join him and they'd sit in the sun together.

'How's it going Dylan?' Gramp would ask, and laugh as Dylan told him how hard he was working.

'It's not funny, Gramp. It's really difficult. I thought you just soaped a car all over, then rinsed it off, but these men are dead fussy. They want mud scraped off the bumpers and the licence plate. They want their wing mirrors dried and their windscreens to be without a single smear. Do you know how long it takes to get all the smears off a windscreen? It's not like I can reach the middle, anyway.'

Gramp's eyebrows were lost in his mop of white hair as he listened. Dylan watched laughter bubbling out of the old man as he pictured Dylan heaving bags of mown grass to compost heaps; carrying bucket after bucket of water from kitchens to cars and scrubbing at gritty bits of muck on parts of cars that were difficult to reach.

Each day as Dylan toiled away he'd save up exaggerated details and look forward to telling them to Gramp and watching him wipe his eyes after his stories were done. One day he remembered to ask a question that had been in his mind for a while.

'What's a crowbar, Gramp?'

'A crowbar? Burglars call them jimmys. They're wrecking bars, for smashing stuff. Essential tool for a burglar. Why?'

'Oh, nothing,' Dylan said.

But he knew it did mean something.

After a week, Dylan had a tan, hard muscles in his arms and legs and a total of one hundred and fifty pounds. Buying a new bike began to seem a real possibility.

Megs already loved him, and once he had got the bike he'd stop working and start building some jumps. It was best not to think about the original bike track. He'd just concentrate on how great it would be to have a mountain bike instead.

Sometimes he would overhear Tommo telling his mum how great Floyd was and how he would play Top Trumps whenever Tommo wanted him to and how he always looked out for him in the group, but mostly Dylan was too busy to think about the others at all.

All the puppies' eyes were open now and they were scampering about, bumping into each other, falling over, jumping up again. Megs was always the first to see him and she rushed towards him each day, trailing her siblings behind her, wagging and snuffling and squeaking. Bella barely stirred when he went to see them, except to lap water and collapse again in her basket.

The puppies were all black, with splashes of white here and there, down the chest or over the head, all full-bellied and short-legged, furry little barrels of milk wobbling around, without knowing where they were going. Dylan sat among them in the sun, letting them climb all over him, picking them up to smell their soft fur and feel their paws pattering all over him.

A puppy with a white nose nudged Megs off, stuck a paw in his ear and scrabbled, trying to find a hold so that it could reach the top of his head. It hurt, but he smiled. He lay down in the sunshine and let them bustle all over him, pulling Megs up to his chest. She crawled up towards his face and licked his chin, wagging so hard she fell over. He sat up and lifted her so they were eye to eye together, and she strained to get closer to lick him more.

The bungalow door banged open and Gramp shuffled out, slower than usual.

'Whassamatter, Gramp?'

Gramp gave a long sigh.

'Not had much luck on the horses, Dylan. Need something to take my mind off it. Tell me something funny, lad.'

Dylan's dad went mental when he heard about Gramp losing money on the horses, so Dylan changed the subject.

'Look Gramp, this is Megs. She can hear me now, watch. Megs?' He called and watched her velvety head tilt towards him. 'See? She knows her name even. I want to teach her to sit when she's older.'

'You can start now, lad.' Gramp told him to place her on the ground, standing up on her four stocky legs. 'Dip your fingers in milk, boy. Then hold them high over her head, so that she has to sit down to tilt her head far enough back. The moment her bottom hits the ground, call out 'sit!' and let her lick your fingers. That's it! Keep at it, lad. She'll soon learn the word and do it without the milk.'

Dylan spent the rest of the day training Megs, who fell over backwards quite a lot, and wandered off with her siblings every now then. Concentration wasn't her strongest point. But by tea-time she'd managed to sit and lick his fingers three times in a row.

'Clever girl!' he said and she leapt up and licked him on the nose.

Chapter 12

At last the only person left to ask was the piano-tuner. Trouble was, his cottage was right next door to the old vicarage and Dylan wasn't keen on listening to everyone having fun in Floyd's garden. But there were still two hours before tea. If he didn't knock on the door, he'd have to spend all afternoon cycling around, pretending to himself that he wanted to be on his own.

The door had a shiny brass knocker which Dylan was just about to bang when he heard howls of laughter coming from next door. He took a deep breath and banged the knocker three times, hard as he could, so that it rang in his ears.

The piano-tuner opened the door with an expression of fright on his face and listened while Dylan offered his services. He moved his head with quick, bird-like movements, as if he was always checking for danger. Shy, his mum called him. At first he said his car was clean and there wasn't much fuel in the lawn-mower. Then he saw Dylan's face and had a change of heart.

'I'm about to go into town anyway, so I'll fill up the petrol container while I'm there and you can come back tomorrow if you like.'

'Perhaps I could make a start with the petrol that's in it? You might be back before it's even run out?'

Dylan hoped he didn't sound as desperate as he felt. The piano-tuner looked unsure, checked the clear blue sky, then shrugged. Said he'd be back in under an hour with more petrol and he supposed Dylan might just as well get started.

He showed Dylan the mower, told him to be sensible and left him to it. Dylan wheeled the mower out of the garage to the lawn and aimed it in a straight line towards the end.

He was half-way through mowing, with a bright, lime green half on his right and a darker, grassy half with dandelions and daisies on his left, when the engine ran out of fuel and cut out. Once the buzzing of the engine had stopped and the ringing echo of it in his ears died down, Dylan could hear them all – they were on the pavement outside the house now.

Their voices came straight through the holly hedge, as if Dylan was right there with them. They were all laughing at something, shrieking and yelling in such a way that Dylan could picture their faces. He listened, trying not to care, trying to pretend it all sounded silly. Then Matt's voice came over the hedge.

'Floyd! Hey, Floyd, get this!' There was a silence, apart from a faint whirring noise, then 'How cool was that? Am I or am I not Mr King Rollerblader? Did you see that, Floyd? Floyd?'

Cheers, clapping and laughter. Then Matt's voice again.

'Anyone want a toffee?'

Dylan put his hands over his ears and closed his eyes. How long could the piano-tuner be? If only he had more petrol, he wouldn't have to listen to any of this.

He sat on the grass with his head in his hands and a finger jammed into each ear for what seemed like ages until the piano tuner tapped him on the shoulder and showed him a full tank of petrol. He was off again in a matter of seconds, buzzing along, creating neat lines of bright green, blissfully isolated in the engine's noise.

He came to the end of the last strip of lawn and turned round to survey the perfect parallel stripes which lay behind him. He was pretty good at it by now. He let the engine run for a bit, dreading turning it off.

When at last he did and the buzzing died away he was surprised by the silence. He stood still, not wanting to move. A car went by on the main road. A sheep bleated and was answered by another in a nearby field. A pigeon fluttered up from some branch. But otherwise, silence. No laughing, no voices.

They must have gone in for tea, Dylan realised, and tilted the mower back on its wheels to push it into the garage. He collected his pay from the piano man, thanked him and pushed his bike up the pavement, too tired to cycle uphill, thinking of his tea and what his mum might have made. Maybe it'd be sausages and mash.

Every bone ached, but with that last fiver he'd

just reached one hundred and eighty pounds. Still a hundred and ten pounds to go. Two more weeks of solid work, four cars or gardens a day on each week day – and he'd be there. He leant on his bike's handlebars and rolled it up the pavement.

Then, glancing ahead, he saw the one person he didn't want to see. Floyd was coming down the pavement towards him, with the others trailing behind. This time Dylan was determined to stand his ground – Floyd could back off or go round for a change, and he could take his stupid hair-do with him.

What an idiot he looked. Today he had a big bump of hair at the front – a bit like that pop star Gramp liked – Elvis Presley. Then Dylan remembered that he himself was covered in bits of grass and probably red in the face, too.

What he couldn't work out was why Floyd was coming down the pavement, when his house was behind Dylan. Then the reason hit him in the face. They'd all been at Matt's for tea, hadn't they?

Floyd marched towards him, as if he was about to speak. Dylan stopped and blocked the pavement with his bike, his front wheel aimed straight at Floyd. This time, Floyd was going to have to budge.

'Get. Out. Of. My. Way,' Dylan hissed.

He moved his bike forwards till it was between Floyd's feet. Floyd didn't move, but turned to the boys behind him.

'See? It's useless.' He faced Dylan again. 'We heard the lawnmower stop. Matt's mum told us to ask you to come for tea. What a joke.'

Behind Floyd, Matt looked disgusted, Tommo looked confused and Aled and Rob's foreheads now had yellowish streaks down the front. Floyd turned on his heel and strode back up to Matt's house with the others following. When he reached the door, he turned and yelled down the pavement at Dylan.

'And by the way – mum said our lawn needs doing. You can start mowing tomorrow – first thing.'

Floyd let the others through the door first, then slammed the door behind him, leaving Dylan seething with fury, standing on the pavement alone, clutching the handlebars on his bike.

Chapter 13

When Dylan reached his house at the top of the hill, a brisk wind was blowing up the valley, bending the tops of trees back and forth, and sending twigs and old leaves skittering about. A wind like that always meant rain was on its way, so Dylan moved Bella's basket in under the shelter of the shed. Then he went to find his mum in her greenhouse to tell her he was starving.

It was always too hot inside the greenhouse – a weird glass world where you couldn't hear the outside world, or see anything except tomato plants and tiny green seedlings.

'Hi Dylan, can you open that? And fill up the seed trays will you, and plant these for me?'

'I'll be dead in about five minutes from hunger, Mum, but if you don't mind a corpse in your greenhouse, that's completely fine with me.'

'This won't take long. Just give me a hand, would you?'

Dylan ripped open the bag and held it by its middle upside down to shake some of the soil out.

'How's the bike fund going, Dyl?' she asked as she showed him how to spread the dark soil over the seedling tray and place the tiny grains, four centimetres apart, one centimetre deep.

'Not bad. I'm about half-way there. What's this we're planting?'

'That?' She checked the seed packet, holding it at arm's length and peering. 'That's perpetual spinach.'

'Perpetual?'

'Great stuff, keeps on growing, over and over – never stops.'

'Spinach! Which never stops growing? You're not serious, Mum?'

'Yup. Lasts all summer.' Dylan made a face of horror, as if he'd seen a ghost. He grabbed his neck and staggered backwards.

'Aaarrrggghh. That'll give me nightmares. You can't ask me to plant some weird mutant spinach which never stops growing.' She smiled, but he went on. 'Have some respect, Mum. Haven't you got spontaneous strawberries, or repeating raspberries, or... or...something that's edible?'

His mum laughed and put her hands on her hips and kept on laughing while he rattled on in mock outrage.

'I've never thought of it like that,' she said, catching her breath for a moment. He watched her laughing, standing there in her wellies and overalls and clunky gardening gloves and felt pretty good.

The first raindrop hit him on the ear as he made his way back to the house. Tommo's laugh and Matt's voice wafted out from a window. They must have finished their tea already. The front door opened, then banged shut. Perhaps they were fed up with Floyd. Perhaps they'd had a fight. Dylan could imagine hanging out with them again, if Floyd wasn't there.

They could all go and play football in the garden like they used to, until the rain came. Or it could be like the time when they kept on playing in the rain, getting wetter and wetter and sliding around in the mud until Mum called them in, cross with the mess they'd made of themselves. Raindrops came faster now, and Dylan jogged up to the front door.

Maybe they could hang out in their bedroom, him and Matt and Tommo, like they always used to, with Tommo begging to play Top Trumps and Matt and him just yattering on the bunks, or making pellets with tissue paper and spit and trying to get them to stick on the ceiling. He ran into the house and down the corridor to their room. He flung open the door, a huge grin on his face.

What he saw wiped it off. They hadn't got fed up with Floyd. They'd brought him with them and there he was, in his room. Floyd was sitting on *his* bunk, turning one of his homemade farmer figures round in his hand.

'What *is* this messed up bit of metal?' Floyd said, holding the farmer upside down.

Words wouldn't come out of Dylan's mouth. Everyone stood still except for Floyd, who dropped the figure on the floor. Dylan looked at them all in turn. Tommo didn't speak, but Matt tried.

'Dylan... we were gonna... do you wanna play... erm...' For once words seemed to fail even Matt.

'You're inviting me to play in my own bedroom, is that it, Matt?' There was a strange silence while Tommo and Floyd looked at each other guiltily.

'Get off my bed.' Dylan said, cold with fury. 'Don't touch my things.'

Dylan marched out and slammed the front door behind him. He leant up against the wall by the drive, his breath coming in furious snorts as the rain poured down, flattening his hair and trickling down his neck. His mum was just coming round the corner, pulling her gloves off.

'Dylan? You look...'

'Mum?' He could hardly speak. 'He's in our house.'

'Ah.'

'With Tommo and Matt.'

'That's alright, isn't it?'

'They're in my bedroom, Mum.'

'But it's Tommo's bedroom, too.'

'Yeah, but Floyd is sitting on my bed, picking up my things.' Surely she would understand how that felt?

His mum straightened up, with one hand on her back and the other holding a glove over her head to keep some of the rain off.

'Dylan, I'm sorry, I should have said. Tommo's having a sleepover tonight. Floyd is staying. I knew you wouldn't like it much, but Floyd's mum has to go to court.'

'To court? What's she done?'

'Nothing, it's something to do with Floyd's dad.'

His mum looked tired.

'So I have to give up my room? Why does he have to come to us? Why can't he go to... Aled and Rob's?'

'You've got your room, Dylan, or your bunk, anyway. He and Tommo are good friends. That's why he wants to come here.' All the laughter and colour drained from her face, but Dylan wasn't going to back down.

'It's your choice, Mum. Tell him to go somewhere else, or I'm off.'

'Dylan – his mum's gone already. What do you mean, you're off?'

'And I'm not coming back!' Dylan shoved his hands deep into his pockets and strode off through the rain, ignoring her calls.

Chapter 14

He banged the door of Nant Bach open and shook himself on the mat, scattering raindrops.

'I'm staying here tonight, Gramp. I'll sleep on the sofa.'

'What? I'm too old for babysitting. Go home, lad.'

'I don't need a babysitter,' said Dylan, 'I'm just not going home. Floyd is sleeping in my room tonight.' Gramp put his book on dogs down on his lap with a long sigh.

'Dylan, your problem with that boy is getting out of hand. You're going to have to get on with him sometime.'

'Get on with him? Don't you see? He's ruined everything, Gramp. EVERYTHING. I can't make the bike track now, Tommo and Matt only want to be with him. He's like... like...'

Dylan searched the room for inspiration. There must be some way of explaining what had happened. He caught sight of the huge jigsaw of different breeds of dogs Gramp had almost finished.

'He's like the wrong piece in a jigsaw – he doesn't fit. He's not meant to be here. Everyone's pretending he's part of the jigsaw, but he's not. There's something weird about him and it's messing everything up.'

Gramp screwed up his eyes as if he was trying to understand and took a step towards Dylan. At last – Gramp would have some sympathy, even if no one else did. Dylan began to feel his eyes water at the thought that someone would understand him. Then he saw a dangerous light in Gramp's eyes and heard a low growl.

'Rubbish, Dylan. Life isn't like a jigsaw puzzle. You think each village has an exact number of pieces which fit together just so? With no room for any more?'

Suddenly Gramp seemed to find it funny. His dark eyebrows traced high arcs above his face, his eyes widened and he let out a crazy bark of a laugh.

'You're dumber than I thought, lad. It's a shifting thing. The whole world shifts, every country, all of Wales – even this village is a shifting thing – there are always new people to get used to. Floyd is here now, he's part of our village whether you like it or not.'

Dylan shoved this appalling idea onto a shelf right in the darkest corner of his brain. He'd think it over later. But there were other reasons.

'He's got a crowbar, Gramp.'

'Has he? Must need to open something, then. They've just moved house, haven't they? Probably lost the key to a trunk or something.'

'He's weird...' Dylan tried to be specific. 'His hair changes the whole time, and he plays with Tommo, who's not even eight yet – why does he want to play with someone younger? And he sneers. Everything he says is a sneer.'

'Yes, but since you haven't bothered even to try and make friends, you don't know why. There might be a good reason. He's just got different habits from you – so what? Your hair looks like a flippin' bird's nest. You saying he should have the same hair as you?'

Dylan folded his arms across his chest and gritted his teeth together so hard his jaw hurt. Gramp was wrong. Everyone was wrong. There was something strange about Floyd, and no one else could see it. He wished Gramp would stop talking, but Gramp kept on at him.

'Pull yourself together, lad, you're just being plain silly.'

Dylan got to his feet and glowered at his grandfather. No one had ever called Dylan silly. Anger was making his eyes go dim, and he blinked.

'Silly?!' He delivered a good kick to the leg of the table with Gramp's huge jigsaw puzzle of dogs on it. The table banged back against the wall, shunting the jigsaw forward, so that it broke apart, sending hundreds of pieces slithering to the floor.

'What? Why are you shouting? Look what you've done! Good god, boy, sit down and get a grip on yourself.'

Gramp knelt with difficulty, propping himself up on the sofa with one hand and picking up the pieces with the other. Dylan watched him, blinking, until his breath calmed down, then knelt down beside him. Bits of dogs – tongues, eyes, fluffy bits that could belong anywhere—were strewn over the place. He picked up the pieces, feeling – he could admit it to himself – sillier than he'd ever done in his life before.

'Come on, then, if you're staying. You can have the back room. I'll ring your mum and make sure it's ok. We'll clear this up, knock up an omelette and watch something on the telly.'

As Dylan lay in bed that night he felt more and more sure he was right about Floyd. There was something wrong, something Floyd was hiding.

Where was Floyd's dad and why did they have so much stuff? Why did his mum have to go to court? The only way to get everyone back to normal was to find out what it was. And Dylan would be the person to do it.

Chapter 15

By the time he woke up, Dylan's questions had multiplied. Why did Floyd change his hairstyle almost every day? What was with the crowbar? Why was Floyd going out of his way to be friendly to Tommo? Maybe his dad was in prison and Floyd was his accomplice, lying low in small country village.

So mowing the lawn was the perfect excuse for having a look around. And today was the perfect day. Floyd would be at Dylan's house and Floyd's mum was away.

Dylan strode straight through the garden gate – after all, no one would question him going into any garden these days. The shed was open and he got the mower out, then stopped what he was doing for a moment.

Floyd's bike was leaning up against the shed, silvery, gleaming in the sunlight, with a skull printed on the seat. Dylan put his hands on the handle bars, squeezed the brakes and lifted the front wheel up. Just to get a feel of it. It was smooth and moved easily, lighter than it looked. But it didn't have hydraulic disk brakes, the tyres and their treads weren't nearly as thick as the Muddy Springer's and he couldn't see anything that could be called a bottle boss.

He smiled, leant it back against the shed and

wheeled the lawnmower around. He'd start mowing, then go inside for a 'drink of water'.

By the time he had finished mowing half the lawn, he was genuinely thirsty. It wasn't even a lie. The grass was still damp after yesterday's rain, and it was slow going with the lawnmower, even with all his weight pushed against it. He tried the big window doors he'd gone in through with Tommo on that first Saturday and was surprised to find they were locked. No one ever locked up around here, unless they were going away on holiday.

Round the side of the house was a narrow alleyway. A couple of metal bins stood beneath a half-open window. He moved one of them under the window and stood on it to get in.

He climbed over the window-sill, and found himself sitting on top of the washing machine. It suddenly began to vibrate, giving him a fright. He jumped off it and made his way along a corridor into the kitchen.

There wouldn't be any secrets in the kitchen, Dylan was sure of that. He was about to walk straight through when he noticed a large photo of Floyd on the fridge. Must have been taken about four or five years ago. In the photo he looked more like a hot chocolate sort of person. With warm, friendly eyes that looked right at you. Could people change that much?

Dylan had never thought about that before. Perhaps one day he wouldn't have fizz in his veins.

He tiptoed out of the kitchen and into the hallway. He reckoned if he had a secret, he'd keep it upstairs in his bedroom. The stairs were bare and creaky and as he went up, he had a thought. What if Floyd's mum had come back late last night? How would he explain being upstairs?

At the top of the stairs were two doors. With his heart hammering at twice the normal rate, he opened one of them. It led into a room with a double bed and a dressing table with a mirror and rollers and hairpins and four pairs of scissors on it. He closed the door and tried the other one. Turning the handle, he opened it and stood in the doorway.

What he saw came as a shock. He'd expected a room full of things – posters, shelves of fancy remote-controlled helicopters, boats, gliders, thick new clothes spilling out of drawers and cupboards, piles of board games and puzzles, all that sort of thing. But Floyd's room was empty.

Apart from the bed and a cupboard, there was hardly anything in it. The walls were bare. Floyd's thick new hoody lay on the bed, along with the white trousers. The same photo of Floyd when he was about seven, in a frame, stood on a wooden table. Trust him to have a photo of *himself* in his bedroom, Dylan thought.

There was also a cycling helmet and a travel book about South America. A pad of paper with a list on it which read: warm clothes, pyjamas, passport, tickets, cash in both currencies. The word 'both' was underlined. Dylan took another step into the room and at that moment, a door slammed shut downstairs.

Footsteps could be heard going from room to room in a hurry. There was a groan, then they started up the stairs. The thump and creak of each step nailed Dylan to the floor in paralysed fear.

His mind clouded over. He couldn't move. The footsteps were near the top now. He had to do something. There was only the cupboard or under the bed. He sprang into action, dived under the bed, scrunched himself up in the far corner, arms wrapped around his knees to make himself as small as possible, and held his breath. Blood pounded in his head so loudly he was sure it would give him away.

The footsteps came into the room and approached the table. Floyd's trainers with the thick undone laces were visible from under the bed. There was a grunt of relief, something was snatched up and the trainers turned as if to leave the room.

Then they turned back.

They just stood there. As if Floyd was listening.

Dylan's lungs were about to burst. He longed to let just a tiny bit of stale air out and tiny bit of fresh air back in again, but he didn't dare. If he breathed at all he would gasp. How could he have risked breaking into Floyd's house? Floyd could see the garden was only half done. He must wonder where Dylan was.

'Dylan?' Floyd's voice was soft, disbelieving. Then

he seemed to laugh at himself. The footsteps turned around and left the room. Then they clumped down the stairs.

Dylan sucked in a huge gulp of air. After a while, a door slammed again and Dylan's arms and legs slumped to the floor.

He crawled out from under the bed, dusted himself off and looked out of the window. Floyd was out on the pavement, striding up the hill, holding his cycle helmet. Dylan took one more look at the list, then retraced his steps downstairs and climbed back out through the window onto the bin.

As he jumped down, the bin lid fell off and crashed to the concrete floor. Dylan crouched in case someone had heard, then remembered that he had a cast-iron reason for being there.

He picked up the lid, but before he could replace it, a pair of yellow rubber gloves with the fingers stained a dark red seemed to beckon to him from the depths of the bin. He slammed the lid back on, grabbed the lawnmower and threw himself into a frenzy of mowing the last patch of grass.

No amount of noise could silence the questions that were running through his head. Blood-stained gloves, a list of things to pack, a book about South America and an empty bedroom.

Dylan was even more sure than before that Floyd had a secret, but had even less of an idea of what it was.

Chapter 16

After finishing Floyd's lawn, Dylan ran up to the puppy shed. Megs knew his step and scrambled out of the box and into his arms when he arrived. Smothering him with licks, all over his face and both ears – she was as thorough as his mum when it came to washing – she snuggled up in the hood of his hoody while he mixed the feed and checked the other puppies.

When the puppies fell asleep, Dylan went over to the bungalow and pushed Gramp's door open. A smell of fried eggs and burnt sugar came from the kitchen. He stepped over a pile of newspapers and moved around awkwardly placed furniture. Grown-ups always shook their heads when they spoke of Gramp and said things like 'lost his way' and 'never found his groove'.

Dylan thought that losing your way had its advantages. Gramp at least had time for talking, which most grown-ups didn't have, and he always said what he thought.

After supper that night, Dylan flung himself on the sofa, then swivelled round and upside down so that his legs hung over the back. That was the other good thing about Gramp. You could sit any old way on any bit of furniture, and he never told you to sit properly, like people normally did, as if furniture came with instructions and a rule book. His grandfather, on the other hand, had slumped so low in the sofa, he was almost horizontal.

'Whassamatter, Gramp?'

'I'm in a pickle, lad. It's those puppies. They need expensive injections and special puppy feed now,' he said. 'And, erm...' Gramp waggled his head from side to side as if trying to see both sides of an argument, and then shook his head, 'I'm skint. Stony broke. Had a bit of bad luck on the horses just lately. The bank won't spit out a single penny when I stick my card in.'

Dylan swivelled round again and sat bolt upright, as if he'd taken a three-year course in sitting on sofas.

'I've got money, Gramp. I could let you have... some.'

'Nah... couldn't let you do that, Dylan. Unless...'

'Unless what?'

'Unless we call it investing. So you give me some money, and when I sell the puppies I give you a share of the profits back.'

They worked out if they sold seven pedigree sheepdog puppies for £350 quid each, they'd make two thousand, four hundred and fifty pounds. Neither of them could speak at the thought of so much money.

'That's if we sell them all.'

They were silent again. Bella was old. She wouldn't have puppies next year.

'Do we have to sell them *all?* We could keep Megs, couldn't we?'

''Fraid we can't, Dylan. Bella and I are both too old for this game. And I'm too old to train a young pup.'

'I could train her!'

'It's more complicated than that. Had a slight argument with the electricity people. Say they're going to cut me off if I don't pay their bill.' Gramp looked confused, as if he couldn't think why they would be so mean.

'Not having a phone suits me down to the ground, but I can't get by without the telly,' he said, glumly.

That evening Dylan took Megs into Gramp's house, let her sit on the sofa with him while Gramp watched another of his westerns. Dylan stroked her ears until she fell asleep in his lap as cowboys and Indians galloped this way and that across the screen. Then, before he went to bed, he put her back in the box with all the other puppies and watched her snuggle up and be lost in the breathing black heap of fur.

Just over a week before Tommo's birthday, his mum rang and said he *had* to come home. For suppers at least, she said.

So Dylan walked into the kitchen at exactly 6.30 pm and sat at his place, without looking at anyone. He ate in silence. The only sound was the constant shushing of the rain, the scraping of forks on plates and their mum putting things away in the cupboards behind them.

He wanted to say something to Tommo. But it had been such a long time, he didn't know how to start.

Chapter 17

After breakfast at Gramp's each day Dylan went back home and hung around by the phone in the hall, in case a buyer rang. Helping Gramp sell the puppies was another adjustment to his plan, but because it meant he'd have the money to buy the Muddy Springer the moment Gramp paid him his share. That exact day he could go into town and buy a gleaming bike with front and back wheel suspension and chunky black tyres with treads a tractor would be jealous of.

At night before he fell asleep, he imagined himself careering through the woods and stream on his new bike, crashing down steep banks, twisting round trees and bouncing over boulders. Every morning he woke from dreams of flying through the air over an enormous jump.

He was just explaining to his mum that he was in business now with Gramp, selling the puppies, that they needed every penny, when the phone's jangling tones rang out through the house. He picked up quickly, ready to tell the buyer what great puppies they were.

It came as a surprise that it was Matt's mum. She asked how he was, in an odd voice, and he knew Matt must have said something.

'Fine, thanks. Mum!' he yelled. He went into

the kitchen, so that he'd hear when she'd finished and be ready in case it rang again. Snatches of her conversation came through the door, and he turned the radio down so that he could hear better.

'That's great she's starting up on her own, but I don't think we can do it at our house, Jane. I'd like to be friendly, but I can't ask her back here. Dylan's been staying at his grandpa's since her boy came over… I know, it's upset the whole village – and you know about Tommo's party… Alright, I'll come over to yours. Wouldn't want to miss out on a free hair-do… And I bring a towel, do I, and some photos of what I'd like?… What fun! Yes, I'm sure Matt's upset. I hardly see Dylan now myself… it's horrible here at the moment. I'll bring some biscuits, okay?' Then she hung up.

The phone rang again. It was a woman. She wanted a puppy. She'd come round about 4pm to choose. Dylan raced up to the shed, yelling for Gramp.

A wave of dark, furry bodies rushed to greet them at the corner of their box. The puppies wagged so hard that sometimes they slipped over to one side. Dylan knelt down and put out his hand. Small pink tongues hurried to lick it.

'I wonder which one she'll choose.'

'We can't let her choose. It's like a marriage, Dylan. We have to help her get the one that'll suit her.'

'So we need to work out what she's like before we suggest which dog she should have?'

'Bingo.'

Dylan stepped into the box and sat down in the straw among the puppies. The one with the white nose, which had stuck a paw in his ear a few weeks ago rushed up to him, pushed Megs out of the way again and scrabbled up his body towards his face.

'She's the top dog, eh, Gramp?'

'Yup, leader of the pack, that one. We'll call her Boadicea,' Gramp said.

'Boadicea?'

'You know, the fearless Celtic Queen who led her army against the Romans. Nearly chased them out of Britain. Didn't manage it, of course. They were here to stay. Don't they teach you anything at school these days?' Megs was following Boadicea up Dylan's chest, but was nosed off by her stronger sibling.

'Look, Gramp, Megs is learning. Sit!' he commanded, and as Megs plomped herself down on her bottom, wagging, Dylan beamed at Gramp. 'See? Isn't she clever?'

Another puppy sat at his feet, not moving as much as the others, a calm little thing, sweet and dozy, black all over, wagging gently. Dylan picked her up.

'So you're the runt, are you? You can be Polly.'

Their first buyer sounded quite old, older than his mum. Maybe Polly, a quiet, easy-going dog, would be right for her.

He changed his mind the moment her car drove through the gate. She came in fast and parked right outside the front door, as if she'd only stopped because the door was too narrow to drive through and she would have liked to park in the kitchen. The car throbbed with music for a moment even after the engine was turned off.

Purple-trousered legs emerged from the driver's door. The purple didn't stop as the rest of her followed – they were dungarees, with a dark pink tee-shirt underneath the straps. She had a stern expression on her face as if she expected to have an argument. There was something unpleasant about her, like one of those coffee-flavoured walnut cakes which you think is going to taste of fudge, but is disgustingly bitter instead. Dylan suspected Polly would be terrified of her.

Dylan led her to the shed with the puppies in. She bent down to snatch up Polly. 'Oh, aren't you a sweetie!' She nuzzled her so hard that Polly squeaked. Gramp was standing by the shed, both hands on his stick. Dylan looked at him and saw he was signalling with one wagging finger and urgent eyes that she must at all costs be prevented from buying Polly.

Her booming voice sounded across the courtyard. 'I need a dog to bark at people. Give 'em a scare.' She took a male puppy from Dylan and gave him a shake, 'and you're gorgeous too, aren't you?' not hard enough to hurt him, but harder than he had ever been shaken before. He stopped wagging for a moment, but took it up again, staggering, once she put him down.

Dylan checked Gramp's face again. This wasn't going well. He didn't feel he could let this poor creature spend the rest of its days with her. That only left Boadicea. He picked her up and raised his eyebrows and Gramp nodded and began to smile.

'This one's got a lot of spirit, miss,' Dylan said. The woman held Boadicea up to her face, close enough for a lick and was bitten, a sharp-toothed puppy bite, on the nose. She burst out laughing. 'Oh, I like you!' she said. She paid in cash, and after kissing the puppy almost to death, placed it in a travel cage in the boot of her car.

They watched her reverse so fast that she knocked a plant pot over. Then she did an energetic three-point turn and stormed through the gate.

'I think they deserve each other,' said Gramp and they both burst out laughing.

Back in the shed they opened another bag of puppy feed and mixed it with milk until it was good and sloppy.

'Gramp? What happens if two dogs want to be top dog?'

'They fight. And the loser is kicked out of the pack.' Gramp looked at Dylan closely. 'But I reckon we can be better than dogs. All that fighting for power is pretty dull. We can just concentrate on what interests us and what we're good at. We don't have to scrabble for position. In fact, in human beings, it's a sign of weakness, not strength.'

Early the next morning, the piano-tuner came and tilted his head this way and that, listening to the puppies, rather than looking at them. He cradled Polly in his long, bony hands, stroking her as if he was playing a slow piece of music. She fell asleep in his arms, and Dylan and Gramp happily sold her to him. Three families came the following day and made their choices. That left only two. Megs and a male puppy.

Chapter 18

A farmer turned up, in a hurry, wanting to get back to harvesting and checked Megs and the male puppy, looking at their teeth, their paws, whistling to make sure they could hear him. It was clearly a difficult decision. Dylan couldn't bear to watch and mumbled something to Gramp and sloped off out of the shed. At last Gramp came tottering into view with his stick. He was brandishing a bunch of notes.

'Here you are lad. He bought the male pup. I'm sure I'll sell Megs – so you can have your share now. We made four times what we paid – there's two hundred quid there. It's all yours, you've earned it.' Dylan grasped the wad of notes in his fist and grinned.

'Thanks Gramp. It was fun, too, wasn't it?' He wandered off and leant against the wall by the shed, counting the notes, amazed at having so much money in his hand.

'I've done it, Megs, look. I told you I would, and I did.' Alone in the puppy box, she wandered around, as if she was looking for her siblings. He sat beside her and she came and jumped into his lap and settled down.

A long, gurgling sniff made him turn round and, looking up, he saw that Tommo was leaning against the wall, wiping his nose with the back of his sleeve.

'Hey Tommo, come and meet Megs. What's the matter? Where's Fashion Model today? Busy fixing his hair?' Tommo's red and blotchy face turned towards Dylan.

'His mum does his hair. She needs to practise. She's starting up a hairdressers...' A pang of guilt slithered through Dylan's mind – so Gramp had been right – there was a good reason for his odd hairstyles. That didn't explain everything though. Tommo was still talking between sniffs.

'... you will come to my party, won't you Dylan?'

'He's ruined everything for you too, hasn't he?' Dylan felt a moment's pity for Tommo, but it didn't last long, because Tommo started screaming at him.

'Don't you get it, Dylan? You're the one who's ruined everything, not him. He's alright – you just never gave him a chance. *You're* the one who won't come to my party. It's all *your* fault.' Tommo smashed his fist against the wall, then whimpered, 'Ow!' and with one last teary look at Dylan, ran off out of the courtyard.

Chapter 19

Two hundred pounds in tenners and fivers rustled in Dylan's hand. One or two notes were clean and stiff, but most were softer, flopped over, bent at the edges. He had more than enough to buy the Muddy Springer bike. He'd done it! At last he could start building some jumps. It wouldn't be the same as a proper bike track, but Dylan tried not to think about that.

Dylan brought Megs up to eye level and kissed her soft head before placing her back in her box, next to Bella. He shoved the notes deep into his back pocket and walked down the hill through the woods to the rope swing and sat on the bank of the stream.

He pictured himself on his new bike, shooting along beside the stream, storming down near-vertical slopes, twisting this way and that through the wood. All he had to do was ask Mum to take him into town. But he kept being distracted from this wonderful vision of himself in the bike shop.

If only Gramp hadn't lost so much money on horses, he'd keep Megs, breed from her. Dylan would have helped. He'd have trained her, fed her, remembered to give her fresh water every day. It wasn't fair – if only he could keep Megs…

At the word 'fair', Gramp's face appeared in his

mind, spluttering with laughter, and he knew what he would say. Stop moping and do something about it!

The stream, much fuller after so many days of rain, swirled past him, hurrying onwards and downwards while he just sat there, stuck in a hopeless situation. Rays of golden afternoon light were coming at him, slanting-ways now, reminding him that the summer was nearly over.

Then, with a slow wave of amazement he realised that he could buy Megs. Right now. Just walk up to Gramp, hand over all the money he'd earned, and she'd be his. His mum and dad would be fine with it – they always had dogs, they'd know that Dylan would look after her well.

For a while he couldn't move. It would be another huge change of plan. There wouldn't be any point in building jumps all on his own without a decent bike. He'd worked so hard for the bike, all summer long. The thought of whizzing along rough ground with full suspension was brilliant – but he knew for certain that he would never know what it was like.

He wanted Megs more than anything. He could breed from her, keep one of her puppies when she was old. A new bike would be fun, but it wouldn't come anywhere near keeping Megs.

He leapt to his feet and ran up the bank. Gramp would be so happy too, he knew he would. By the time he reached the shed, he was out of breath, wild with excitement, longing to tell someone, everyone.

But when he got there, the box was empty and Gramp was sitting on an upturned barrel, his head in his hands.

'Gramp?'

'Oh, Dylan!' Gramp looked as if betting on horses had been cancelled forever.

'What's the matter? Where's Megs? I've come to buy her, Gramp – I don't want the bike, I've made my mind up!'

'Oh, Dylan!' Gramp's voice sounded terrible, as if someone had died. Then Dylan had an awful thought.

'Something's happened to Megs – what's happened, is she all right?'

'Your mother... she knew you were saving up... She knew we needed the money. She thought you'd be pleased. She sold her, Dylan. She sold Megs.' He let his head sink into his hands again.

'No! We can get her back, say there's been a mistake, say...' But Gramp had lifted his head and was staring at him as if there was worse to come.

'Floyd's mum came with her, Dylan. She sold her to Floyd.'

Chapter 20

Dylan sat in his place at supper that night as if he were made out of stone. He stared at his fork, knowing he was supposed to do something with it. The brown lumps on his plate looked familiar but he couldn't imagine why anyone would bother eating.

He didn't notice that Tommo's head hung over his plate, or that his mother's lips were pressed together, as if she was trying to keep something in. She hadn't spoken since he came in through the door, yelling 'How could you do that?' As soon as she'd realised how angry he was, she'd stopped talking altogether.

Usually it was great when the weather meant Dad was home in time for supper, but this evening they sat in silence, listening to the rain and the wind smashing against the windows and eating their meatballs and spaghetti methodically, like sheep chewing grass.

Dylan managed to lift his eyes to his mum's. They stared at each other for a moment, then she went bright red, her shoulders slumped, and she stopped eating. She was still, in essence, a strawberry – but a very squashed one. She looked as if she was going to cry.

'What's the matter, love?' his dad asked, putting an arm on her shoulder as it heaved up and down. She shook her head.

'Everything,' she said. 'I've just sold Dylan's favourite puppy to the one person he would never have sold it to. Matt's mum's hardly talking to me, and Tommo and Dylan don't laugh – don't even talk anymore – everything's gone wrong and I can't understand it...'

There was a long silence. Dylan felt horrible, as if it was his fault in some way, but he couldn't think how. He prodded a meatball with his fork and lifted it to his mouth. It tasted of nothing. Could grief make you lose your sense of taste?

For days he lived like a robot. He had the same body, the same hands and face, but he felt empty, as if his body was just a shell, without him inside it. He missed Megs so much, it hurt. Fizz was something he couldn't even remember. The pile of notes was useless now – but being busy was better than doing nothing, so he kept on working and going to market to sell figures and the money kept rolling in.

The Wednesday before Tommo's birthday, he walked past the toy stall again in the market and bought the red Lamborghini. It gave him a moment's pleasure before he sank back into his gloom again.

At tea that evening, his dad told him to snap out of it.

'Go and see Megs. Ask Floyd if you can take her for walks sometimes or something. But for goodness sake pull yourself together, Dylan.'

'Do I have to?'

'Yes. This evening. As soon as you've finished.'

'Floyd says she's not eating much, Dylan. He thinks maybe he's doing something wrong. He's worried about her.' It was the first time Tommo had spoken to Dylan for a week.

After tea, which he mostly left on his plate, he walked out of the house and down the hill. He felt programmed, robotic. His legs took him to Floyd's house. He didn't know what he'd say when he got there, and he didn't care how much Floyd sneered at him and taunted him, he just had to see Megs, make sure she was okay.

He knocked on the front door, half in a dream. Floyd opened it and behind him in the hallway Dylan saw Megs lying curled up in a wicker dog basket. It seemed odd that the knocking hadn't woken her. He didn't bother saying 'hi', he just went straight to the point.

'Can I see Megs? I could take her for a walk if you like. I mean, if it's raining or something, I could take her for walks quite a bit. Dad and Tommo said it might help.' He waited for Floyd to sneer at him.

But Floyd didn't sneer. He half turned away, then wheeled back and asked in his drawly voice, 'Could you just shut up about your dad and your brother? Right from the start – my dad's got the farm on the hill... my dad's been here for six generations... my brother and I – you never stop, do you?'

Dylan gaped. What was he on about? But Floyd hadn't finished.

'It's great for you, you've got everything. And you have to shove it in people's face, *my* this, *my* that, *my* everything.'

'*I've* got everything?' Dylan's voice rose to a shout of surprise and woke Megs, who scrabbled out of her basket and looked around, madly.

'Doesn't mean you have to go on and on about it.'

'Whaddya mean *I've* got everything? *You're* the one with the playroom like a toyshop.' Now Floyd did sneer, a bitter, sarcastic sneer as Megs rushed past him and scrambled up Dylan's legs.

'Yeah, like anyone cares about plastic toys.' His voice became a drawl again and for the first time Dylan heard sadness in the low tones. 'I mean your dad. And your brother – not that you care about him. I bet you just use him all the time and he does anything you want. Your farm, your life, everything's just right for you, isn't it?' Dylan struggled to work out what Floyd was talking about at the same time as containing Megs's excitement.

'Is your dad… do you…?' Megs was licking him all over his face, but he was so surprised he couldn't concentrate on her.

'Left us. A few months ago. Lives in Brazil now. He… he took my brother with him. And emptied the bank account.'

Floyd suddenly stared up at the turquoise evening sky as if he wasn't having a conversation at all. 'It was his tenth birthday that day you first bumped into me. My mum keeps trying through the courts, but I reckon I won't see him for years. All I've got is a photo of him in my bedroom.' Floyd's voice got even slower. 'Sometimes I'm so angry I go out and hit things.'

Neither boy spoke for a few moments and only the trilling of a single bird broke the silence. Then Floyd carried on.

'That's why I've got two of everything. Mum wouldn't let me tell anyone when we arrived. Said it was like asking for sympathy. But I can't stand listening to you going on and on.'

Floyd's face was red and his dark eyes were glistening. 'I used to be like you – didn't really care about anyone. You just take Tommo for granted, don't you? I bet this summer is the first time in his life he hasn't done exactly what you wanted.' Then his jaw was clenched tight, as if it couldn't let another word out.

'I didn't know... I...' stammered Dylan.

'How could you? As if you'd give anyone a second chance. And you can give Megs back.' He held his arms out and after one last hug, Dylan passed her over, his mind reeling.

Then Floyd turned and closed the door behind him, leaving Dylan standing on the mat.

Chapter 21

Dylan walked away from Floyd's house, towards the old oak tree with leaden shoes. He leant back against its solid trunk and slid his back down to meet his heels, crouching there, immobile, staring at the dry earth and its littering of acorns, twigs and pebbles.

All his plans were ruined. None of his friends would ever speak to him again. Buying a bike seemed pointless now. Without Megs he didn't care about the bike or making jumps. The whole summer was wasted.

He ran through all that had happened, over every scene and felt the heat creep up his cheeks. It was simple. Tommo had been right. Quite a lot of it was his own fault.

On the morning of Tommo's birthday Dylan woke late. Gramp was nowhere to be seen. He rushed across the courtyard but there was no one at home, either. The party was starting soon. He didn't want to go, but he couldn't keep away.

He didn't want to be seen hanging around so he kept back a bit, by the oak tree. He reached up to the lowest branch. He curled his hand around it and pulled himself up with tanned, muscular arms. He settled himself in two branches which formed a seat and sat in the cool dappled sunlight, peering through the leaves at the village hall door and waited.

His mum and Matt's mum appeared, laden with plastic bags, each trying to persuade the other to go in through the door first. He was sure they never used to be so polite to each other.

A car drove up and parked on the kerb and a load of children Dylan knew from Tommo's class spilled out, and ran towards the village hall door. Then Tommo himself turned up, with Matt, Floyd, Aled and Rob and disappeared inside. Then in went Floyd's mum – with dyed red hair. He groaned at his suspicions over the yellow gloves stained with what looked like blood.

Through the open door came the steadily building noise of children's voices, and the louder it got, the smaller and colder Dylan became, until he'd shrunk into himself, hugging his folded knees. He knew what he had to do. Just one thing for Tommo. He had to go to his party and look as if he was enjoying it.

Dylan climbed down from the tree and ran home to wrap up Tommo's present. After that, he'd keep away from them all – it didn't matter, he had plenty to keep himself busy. But he had to try to make Tommo's party a good one.

He took his bike and freewheeled down the hill. Maybe his brakes would give out and he'd crash before he got there in a terrible accident. Then everyone would feel sorry for him instead of fed up with him. But his brakes brought him safely to a stop just outside the village hall.

With his heart thumping in his throat, he leant his bike up against the wall and peered in under the plastic banner with the words HAPPY BIRTHDAY in rainbow colours, which his mum put up over the door for every birthday.

He tried to look in without being seen, like a policeman in a shoot-out. Half the table was visible, all laid out with matching cups and plates and napkins, all with bicycles on. He inched his nose a little further round the door and saw his mum, and aunt, and Matt's mum and Floyd's mum, all holding cups of tea and standing around, smiling as if they didn't know what to say. No one noticed him standing there.

He edged further round, ready to pull back if anyone turned their head. He could just see the back of Tommo's head in the middle of the group of children, ripping off wrapping paper and calling out, 'Hey Mum, look, a dart board, thanks, Matt,' in a voice that didn't sound quite right.

A blue ribbon flew up into the air as Tommo flung it over his shoulder. Dylan watched it flutter down among noises of admiration from Tommo's friends over a present he couldn't see.

Something was wrong. Something was missing, though he couldn't work out what it was, from where he stood. He searched the room, checking the details. Balloons bobbed from every window and streamers wafted in the breeze.

Then he caught sight of Floyd, handing Tommo a present, smiling, looking really friendly. Tommo took the present and said 'Thank you'.

Floyd turned suddenly and caught Dylan looking at him. His face went back to the way it had been that first day when Dylan and Tommo had gone to ask him for a ride. It was stiff and unfriendly and he stuck his chin out and ran his hand through his hair. Dylan pulled back behind the door. He stood there, watching Floyd's expression change again in his imagination and understood. Floyd had been frightened of him.

He took a huge breath, tried to ignore the thumping which had now reached his ears and pushed the door open. He walked up to the group surrounding Tommo, which fell silent and turned to look at him. Matt's freckled face was unreadable and Floyd looked away but Tommo's face lit up with delight, filling Dylan with another pang of guilt.

'Hey Tommo, happy birthday,' he said, handing him the huge present.

Tommo looked at him, still with a hopeful expression on his face and Dylan managed to smile.

'Alright if I come after all, Tommo? Hope I haven't missed the cake?'

He slid a glance at Matt, who still hadn't changed his expression. He tried Floyd.

'Hi, Floyd,' he said, hoping he was right, hoping it would work. Floyd shrugged.

'Hi there,' he answered, looking down at his feet,

beginning to grin. Shreds of wrapping paper drifted through the air as Tommo ripped it off the box. When it lay in tatters at his feet, Tommo didn't speak for a while, just stared through the see-through plastic at the red Lamborghini inside. Then he looked up at Dylan with shining eyes.

'Cor, thanks, Dylan,' he said, as if he hadn't enough breath to say it.

'It's remote control,' Dylan pointed out. The thumping in his ears had stopped. Tommo's face was so amazing, Dylan felt a few moments of soaring happiness.

The mothers must have all finished their cups of tea at the same time, because they were everywhere, telling them all to sit down, handing round hot party sausages, plate after plate of crisps, cheese straws, nuts, slices of pizza and sandwiches.

Everyone was yelling and grabbing handfuls of food and piling their plates up high with iced biscuits and brownies and marshmallow snowballs and hula-hoops. Tommo was sitting between Floyd and Aled who were stealing food from each other's plates and pretending they didn't know where all the sausages had gone and shrieking with laughter.

Whatever it was that had been missing, wasn't missing anymore. Tommo's birthday cake came in – his mum had made a huge chocolate cake decorated like a car wheel with spokes in silver icing and a chocolate tread around the edge.

Half-way through listening to everyone sing 'Happy Birthday' Tommo stood up and put his hands on his hips, grinning all over his face. The moment they stopped he yelled,

'I'm eight! Yeah!' in his old voice, which made everyone laugh except, Dylan noticed, his mum, who was crying instead. He heard Matt's mum say,

'What's happened?' and his own mum answer, laughing through her tears,

'I don't know!'

Once the games were over and the mothers had begun to tidy up flabby bits of left over pizza, Dylan couldn't help looking at the door. Soon, he could leave.

Chapter 22

Dylan walked his bike up the hill from the village hall, watching the lines of the kerb slide by. It was an effort to put one foot in front of the other. Running, cycling and rollerblading seemed insane activities. He could hear the others coming out of the village hall; it sounded as if they were going down the hill towards Floyd's house.

When he reached the courtyard, he stopped. He knew it would hurt him to see the empty box again, but it seemed the only place to go. He rounded the corner and saw Bella, lying in the sun. She jumped up to greet him, with more energy than he'd seen all summer.

'Pups all gone, hey, Bella? Guess that means some rest for you.' She licked his hand and wagged and he knelt down to bury his face in the fur around her neck, and stroke her hard.

Cries came up the hill behind him. There was no escaping Floyd and the others – they would always be all over the village. Dylan saw the next few years stretching ahead of him and realised that Gramp was right, Floyd was part of the jigsaw now.

What were they shouting? They weren't calling each other's names, like they usually did. What was it? It was his name, and they were yelling it madly –

and another – was it Megs? Were they teasing him? Taking Megs out and calling to him to watch? A flicker of anger came to life and he stood up and walked around the wall.

Whatever they were doing, they weren't teasing. They were panting, yelling, running as fast as they could up the hill after a huge birthday tea. Matt arrived first.

'Dylan, it's Megs – she ran off. She came this way – up towards your house. She hasn't eaten anything for two days – she'll be really weak, and we can't find her.'

'Why hasn't she eaten? What were you feeding her?' Dylan turned to Floyd, who'd just caught up.

'Same stuff you'd been feeding her – it wasn't that. I dunno why she wouldn't eat. Mum said she was pining.'

'Which way did she go?'

'She bolted up the hill towards your house, but the last I saw of her was when a car started up. I think it frightened her – she ran off into the woods by the stream. She could be anywhere by now! We just thought...'

'Thought what? She's your dog, Floyd. You sort it out.'

'Mum thinks she was pining for you, Dylan. We thought the sound of your voice might bring her back.'

Floyd's face went scarlet as he said this, but he

managed to look Dylan in the eye. Dylan broke into a run, feeling more alive than he had done for days. Floyd tried to keep up with him, and Tommo and Matt followed close behind.

The boys rushed down the road, calling, searching. She was so small and dark, she could be nestling by a tree root and they'd hardly see her. Dylan used his eyes like tools, checking every dark patch, every large leaf, methodically, nudging logs with his toe to make sure he didn't miss her.

'Megs!' he called, over and over. They'd come to the rope swing where it hung above the stream. After all the rain the stream was full of tumbling water. It rushed past, full of wild energy, impatient to escape the land and reach the sea.

The boys stopped and stared at the swirling water. No one spoke. Water rushed along, crashing into boulders, leaping up and bubbling and careering onwards. A grassy bank overhung the water's edge. Even Bella wouldn't have been able to clamber out there, let alone Megs.

'Hey!' Tommo was pointing, upstream, towards the fallen tree trunk. 'Is that her? It is, it is!'

Dylan searched – did he mean the bank? The stream itself? He couldn't see her anywhere.

'Where, Tommo, where?'

'There, on the tree – the one that fell across the river!'

Then Dylan saw her – crouched on the trunk right

in the middle of the river, backed up against a bit of branch that pointed up into the air. She was shaking, wet from the spray, and looked even smaller than when he'd last seen her.

'Megs!' he cried and she turned her head towards him. She tried to stand up.

'No! Wait! Sit!' Dylan was glad he'd started to train her. Then he remembered – she wasn't his. He looked at Floyd.

'Floyd?' he said, though it killed him not to rush over and gather her up himself. But Floyd didn't move.

'I can't.'

'What do you mean, you can't? She can't come back on her own, can she?'

'No, but I just can't. I can't climb along the tree, Dylan.

'But she'll die if you leave her...'

'Dylan! She's slipping!' Tommo's voice screeched out, and Dylan saw that she'd tried to wobble towards him.

One paw was sliding down the mossy trunk and each time she tried to bring it up, it slid down again. Her tiny red tongue showed as she panted and her eyes pleaded for Dylan to come to her.

Dylan pushed past the boys and ran towards the tree trunk. She must have crawled along one of the branches and he stepped over them, seeing everything from Megs's eyes.

She would have used that tiny branch to push up from; she'd have pattered along the bark, where her paws could get some grip. She must have been so frightened to come along here. He made his way between the branches and sat astride the trunk, fixing her with his eyes and talking to her over the noise of the rushing water, hoping his voice would calm her, buy him some time.

He inched his way along, placing his hands on the trunk and heaving himself forward, not wanting to go so fast that he jogged the trunk, nor to go so slowly that he got there too late. He could hear her whimpering now and she was wagging, straining her neck towards him. Her front paw was slipping and the back legs were beginning to slide, too.

Dylan placed his hands on the broad trunk and pulled himself forwards, heaving and sliding, heaving and sliding, his eyes locked on hers, with the shouts of the others a million miles away behind him.

'No!' he cried, as she finally lost her grip. He lunged forward, grabbed the branch she'd been crouching by for balance and flung his other hand out as she fell, feeling her soft fur brush by his fingers.

He grabbed at it, caught the loose fold of white fur around her neck between the knuckles of his middle and fourth fingers and gripped tight, pulling her towards him. It was such a slight grip, such a small amount of fur caught between his knuckles that he felt sure the weight of her would pull her down and away. He gripped as tightly as he could, squeezed his eyes shut, as if that would help, and drew her towards him, reaching under her with his other hand.

Dylan was lying face down on the trunk, at full stretch, but he had her cupped in both hands, safe, warm, snuggled into his neck and he lay there for a few seconds, blinking his eyes dry before the others saw him.

It was as if the sound came on again and their cheers surprised him. He kissed Megs, put her in the hood of his hoody and backed up along the trunk, ripping his trousers as he went.

Back on the bank, everyone was jumping up and down and yelling. It was odd to see them all smiling at him and he found it wasn't too hard to smile back. He took Megs out of his hood and lifted her up to his face. She licked and wagged and licked and wagged and Dylan laughed to see her so madly affectionate.

Only Floyd was silent, staring at Megs.

'She's never done that to me,' he said.

Dylan pulled Megs away from his face. He rubbed her against his cheek one last time. He would always love her, but she was Floyd's and for the first time he accepted that without anger. Floyd had lost his father and his brother. He'd even spent a whole summer with embarrassing hairstyles just to help his mum. If anyone deserved a puppy, it was him. He held her out to Floyd, unable to speak. But Floyd didn't take her.

'She'd have drowned if it weren't for you.'

'She's your dog, Floyd, take her.'

'No, Dylan, I don't think she is really my dog. Ok, so we bought her, but she was miserable without you. I would rather start again with another puppy.' He managed a smile.

'She's yours, Dylan, I mean it. I'll tell my mum – we'll sort it out with the money and everything. But she should be with you.'

Chapter 23

Mud spurted up from under Matt's bicycle tyre, splattering Dylan and transforming his green trousers instantly into army-patterned combat gear.

'Go *on*!' Dylan yelled, knowing encouragement wasn't necessary. Matt hunched over the handlebars, pedalling hard with long strides, gathering speed for the ramp ahead. They'd all spent every minute of the last week of the holidays building the track, working as a team, planning and discussing and adjusting their ideas.

Scavenging old doors and planks from garages and rolling massive rounds of tree trunk all the way from their dads' woodsheds, Matt, Dylan and Floyd had constructed one jump which took off from the ground and ended at shoulder level. The idea was to go up it so fast that you'd fly before crashing to the ground and racing off at top speed again. They'd made a zigzag slalom using fence posts and a path along single planks – if your wheel slipped off the plank, you'd be disqualified.

Further on, they'd laid an old door over three bags of fertilizer, with a ramp up. The fertilizer bags acted like beanbags, and the door wobbled, but that was the point.

Aled and Rob had been on sawing duty – getting

rid of all the branches and roots sticking out of the fallen tree trunk, while Tommo, Floyd and Dylan had spent every evening packing the ends with mud and straw to make a solid ramp up to it. Matt had gone silent when they built up the approach to the tree trunk. If Dylan didn't know him better, he'd have suspected him of being afraid.

They had been long days for Megs, who had spent them either trotting around after Dylan, dozing in the sun, or snuggling up in his hood. She was eating like a horse and growing ganglier every day.

But the days were too short for Dylan. Every evening the sun slid below the horizon a little earlier and he had worried that they wouldn't finish in time. He'd spent all his money buying Megs back from Floyd's mum, so he still only had his old bike. But it didn't matter. He worked out he'd have earned enough by Christmas to buy the Muddy Springer.

It had been a funny old summer for plans, but at this precise moment Dylan couldn't see how things could have worked out any better.

Now, at last, on the evening of the last day of the summer holidays, the bike trail was ready and Dylan had been checking the ramp was stable when Matt set off. Matt shot up the first plank, kept pedalling up the second, reached the top of the jump and flew into the air, howling with excitement.

Dylan held his breath – the bike was tipping forward – and if Matt lost control, he'd go head over the handlebars and plant himself in the mud. The front wheel hit the ground and Matt pulled back and started pedalling again, getting into balance and tearing off down the track.

'Yes!' yelled Dylan. 'Next!' He stood back as Tommo came hurtling along on his new bike, then Floyd a few moments later, grinning at Dylan and taking one hand off the handlebars to do a high five as he passed. Now that they were friends, something odd had happened. It was as if Floyd and Dylan had swapped some of their blood. Floyd's icicle had shrunk and had softer edges. Sometimes he even had some fizz about him. Dylan, on the other hand, felt he'd cooled down a bit. At least enough to think before he spoke. He watched Aled, then Rob, shoot off up the ramp, then ran back to the track's start and scrabbled to pick his bike up.

His go at last. So the jump was ok – good and solid. He knew the slalom would be fine. There was a chance the door might wobble him off, but what he was worried about was the tree trunk across the river. They'd done such a good job that there was a clean run up to it, but the closer he got to cycling over it, the less sure he felt.

Driving his pedals hard, he flew over the jump, landing neatly, back wheel first, then raced on to the slalom. He zigzagged along the narrow planks, controlling his wheel to within millimetres of the edge. Deciding there was less chance of wobbling if he went fast, he took the ramp up to the door at speed, and was over.

He headed off towards the stream, hoping there was enough time before his mum called them in, telling him and Tommo they needed an early night, with school starting tomorrow.

Purple stripes were emerging in the sky ahead and the blue was darkening. Quick black flickers in the sky told him the bats were out – chasing this way and that after millions of midges.

He wondered if anyone had bottled out of crossing the tree trunk – or worse, fallen off. He was sorry not to be the first to do it but he was trying hard not to be first these days.

Racing past a line of beech trees, he came to the place where the bank dipped and the tree had fallen straight across. He was surprised to see them all on this side of the stream still, standing by their bikes, leaving a clear path onto the trunk. Suddenly he understood – they'd *all* bottled out. None of them had dared cycle across the fallen tree.

He was pelting along so fast that there were only a few seconds to choose. He could pedal for his life and just hope he'd make it. The stream was full and fast underneath – he'd get soaked through if he fell in, and it wouldn't do his bike any good. But a huge energy came surging up inside him and he aimed his bike straight at the tree trunk, aware of gasps on either side, calls of encouragement, and kept on pedalling so he didn't have to think. He aimed his wheel at a groove of bark, but at the last moment he changed his mind and turned, skidding, splattering mud up at the group of howling, laughing boys.

'Hey!'

'Whaddya do that for?!'

'I'm covered in mud!'

'You chickened out!' called Matt. Dylan grinned at them all.

'Chickened out? Wised up, you mean. You'd have to be stupid to try a thing like *that*.'